Christmas Hotel

Miracle at Christmas Hotel

Christmas Hotel

Miracle at Christmas Hotel

by

Saundra Staats McLemore

Christmas Hotel

Miracle at Christmas Hotel

Christmas Hotel Series Book One

By
Saundra Staats McLemore

Paperback ISBN: 978-0-9826750-4-5

Also available as an eBook
eBook ISBN: 978-0-9826750-3-8
First published by
Desert Breeze Publishing 2012

This new and revised edition

Content Editor: Chris Wright
Cover Artist: Gemini Judson

Scripture Quotations are taken from the King James Version of the Holy Bible

Published by
Well of Life Publishing
Ohio
United States of America

http://www.saundrastaatsmclemore.com

Other Books by Saundra Staats McLemore

The Staats Family Chronicles Series

Abraham and Anna – Book One of Staats Family Chronicles Series – Available now

Joy Out of Ashes

Book Two of Staats Family Chronicles Series

Available now

Christmas Hotel Series

Christmas Hotel (New edition)
Available November 22, 2018

Christmas for Lucy (New edition)
Available December 06, 2018

Christmas Redemption (New edition)
Available December 20, 2018

Christmas Pact (New edition)
Available October, 2019

Christmas Love and Mercy (New edition)
Available November, 2019

Christmas Hotel Reunion (New edition)
Available November, 2019

Dedication

I dedicate Christmas Hotel to my mother-in-law Nettie Sue Harris McLemore. From the Bible's Book of Ruth, she is the Naomi to my Ruth.

Acknowledgements

I would like to thank our Lord and Savior, Jesus Christ for the inspiration He provides for every story I write.

I thank Franklin, Kentucky historian, Gayla McClary Coates, for her very detailed information regarding Franklin, Kentucky in 1941 and 1883. She graciously answered my questions, and much of the information I was able to use for the accuracy of pertinent information in *Christmas Hotel.*

I would like to thank Joseph Palmer, Susan Rieder and Tony Staats for reading *Christmas Hotel* to help find all those annoying little typos!

As always, I thank my husband Robert E. McLemore for his complete support, as I enjoy the passion I have for writing.

I would like to offer a special thank you to Sid and Jill Broderson for granting me permission to have my character Christopher Wright reside in their historical home at 210 South College Street Franklin, Kentucky. This beautiful home is known in Franklin as the "Montague House" or the "Malone House." William Clement Montague built the Italianate structure circa 1860.

Another special thank you to Barbara Beasley Smith for allowing me to have her father Dr. L.F. Beasley "visit" the story.

Chapters

Chapter One

The Journey

"Come unto me, all ye that labour and are heavy laden, and I will give you rest. Take my yoke upon you, and learn from me; for I am meek and lowly in heart: and ye shall find rest unto your souls. For my yoke is easy, and my burden is light."
Matthew 11:28-30

Monday
December 15, 1941
Jerilyn Marlene Seifert gazed out the train window as the countryside passed by. A light snow fell earlier, and the rooftops of the houses now held a thin film shimmering in the sunlight. In the early hours of the morning it had been raining, but she guessed the temperature had now dropped at least fifteen degrees, and she could see icicles forming on the ledge above her window. The treetops glistened with the snow and ice clinging to the branches, bending from the weight. The houses looked so friendly and welcoming.

She watched children running and playing in the snow; dogs barking at their heels. At another house, a woman stood outside ringing the bell to call the family in to the noon meal. Smoke plumed from the chimneys and life was being lived.

Jerilyn shivered and pulled her lap robe up closer to her chin. A steward passing by offered her hot coffee and she smiled as she accepted the cup. Across the aisle, an old couple read their Bibles. The woman next to her was trying to comfort her crying baby. While holding the baby with one arm, she fumbled in her bag with her other hand and pulled out a pacifier. The baby accepted it and began to suck on it contently.

Jerilyn wished that something so simple could give her tranquility. She wondered if she would ever again enjoy inner peace. Her hand cupped her stomach. The delight she had felt for this new life growing inside her was no more. She had never endured such despair in her twenty years. Ken, the love of her life was gone, and she could not believe she would ever feel happiness again.

Jerilyn knew the devastating wording of the telegram would surely stick in her memory forever. She closed her eyes in remembrance.

MRS. KENNETH ADAM SEIFERT
437 NORTH WOODWARD AVENUE DAYTON OHIO
THE NAVY DEPARTMENT DEEPLY REGRETS TO INFORM YOU THAT YOUR HUSBAND

PHARMACISTS MATE FIRST CLASS USN WAS KILLED IN ACTION IN THE PERFORMANCE OF HIS DUTY AND IN THE SERVICE OF HIS COUNTRY. THE DEPARTMENT EXTENDS TO YOU ITS SINCEREST SYMPATHY IN YOUR GREAT LOSS. ON ACCOUNT OF EXISTING CONDITIONS THE BODY IF RECOVERED CANNOT BE RETURNED AT PRESENT. IF FURTHER DETAILS ARE RECEIVED YOU WILL BE INFORMED. TO PREVENT POSSIBLE AID TO OUR ENEMIES PLEASE DO NOT DIVULGE THE NAME OF HIS SHIP OR STATION.

REAR ADMIRAL JACOBS THE CHIEF OF NAVAL PERSONNEL.

"Franklin, Kentucky!" the steward bellowed.

Jerilyn opened her eyes. After boarding the train in Dayton, Ohio, in the wee hours of the morning, the train had made one stop in Cincinnati. Later, she changed trains in Louisville, Kentucky to the L & N Railroad to complete her journey to Nashville. She had enough money for food and lodging for one week, and with her office skills she expected to find work as soon as she arrived. Nashville was a large city, and the original home of her husband. She thought if she met his aunts, uncles, and cousins, she would sense a nearness to Ken. She might find closure. She knew she could not continue in her present state of mind.

The train's wheels ground to a halt. Her legs were cramped from sitting so long, and she hoped to get a snack to tide her over until she reached Nashville. She pulled her only suitcase from the overhead compartment and gingerly walked down the steps, feeling a little wobbly from sitting so long and from lack of eating. The inside of the station was small, but it appeared clean. A beautifully decorated Christmas tree stood in the center, with holly and strung cranberries over each limb, along with lights, decorative bulbs, and artificial icicles. She noticed the diner inside the station, but headed first to the ladies room.

The stop was only for twenty minutes, so she knew she would need to rush. She washed her hands, picked up her bag, and hurried to the diner.

Perching herself upon a stool and setting her suitcase on the floor, she propped her feet protectively on top of the suitcase. A large HELP WANTED sign hung on the wall in front of her. Jerilyn scanned the menu. The smiling young lady behind the counter approached her. The name embroidered on her uniform said Nettie Sue, and Jerilyn decided she looked to be about her age, or maybe a year or so younger.

Jerilyn ordered the chicken salad sandwich with

a glass of water. Having only enough money for one week, she realized she would need to be frugal. She ate hastily, presuming she had maybe five minutes remaining. She slipped off the stool, knelt down, and opened the suitcase. She remembered packing her purse containing her wallet inside, on top of her clothes, but it was nowhere to be found. In a panic, she rummaged through the contents. The purse was gone.

"Is there a problem?" her waitress asked, as she leaned over the counter.

Jerilyn stared up in horror. "My purse is missing," she managed to say. "All my money is in it."

"All aboard! Last call!" the steward announced.

"That's my train!" said Jerilyn, overwhelmed with a feeling of panic.

"I'll get the manager," offered Nettie Sue, and hurried into the back room.

Before the manager emerged, Jerilyn watched the passengers finish boarding, and then the train pulled away from the station. She slumped back down on the stool. *How did this happen? I was so careful with my purse and suitcase.* She thought back to an incident on the first train. When she boarded in Dayton, a man had placed his well-worn suitcase beside hers. She wondered at the time why he set it so close, as there were plenty of other empty compartments. He left the train in Cincinnati. She realized he must have opened her suitcase, snatched her purse, and put it in his suitcase, unbeknownst to her or anyone else. *How can I possibly be so naïve!*

A man walked up to her. With a kind smile, he said in a soft southern drawl, "Nettie Sue told me you have a problem. How may I help you?"

Jerilyn buried her face in her hands, sighed, and began to cry. Nettie Sue stepped from around the counter and placed a comforting arm around her.

"My purse was in that suitcase," Jerilyn said, pointing toward the suitcase still open on the floor. "It contained all my money and now I have none. I was on my way to Nashville, and my train just left. I don't even have money to pay you," she said feebly, "let alone the money for a place to stay. I was going to find work as soon as I arrived in Nashville. Now I don't have the money to get there."

"What's your name, young lady?" the manager inquired, handing her his handkerchief.

"Thank you, sir," she said, as she accepted the monogrammed handkerchief. "Jerilyn Seifert," she answered in a weak voice, while dabbing at her eyes.

"My name is Jonathan Blakely."

Mr. Blakely took a pencil and a small tablet from his shirt pocket and began to write. When he finished, he tore off the paper and handed it to Jerilyn. "There's a friendly hotel in this town that will assist you with a place to stay. It's called Christmas Hotel and the proprietors are friends of mine, Captain and Mrs. Bazell. Just give them this paper. As far as work goes, I can help you with that problem, too. I need someone to work with Nettie Sue. If you're interested, you can stop back here first thing tomorrow morning."

Jerilyn shook hands with Mr. Blakely and hugged Nettie Sue. "I don't know what to say except thank you."

She re-latched her suitcase and Mr. Blakely walked her to the door. Nettie Sue returned to her other customers.

Mr. Blakely pointed up the street. "Just walk two blocks up East Cedar Street and you'll see Christmas Hotel on the corner of East Cedar and North Main Street. It takes up the entire corner, but the entrance is on North Main across from the square. God bless you, Jerilyn. You are in the Lord's hands and you'll be just fine." He patted her arm supportively.

I'm not so sure He cares about me, she thought with unease.

Chapter Two

Christmas Hotel

"Hope deferred maketh the heart sick: but when the desire cometh, it is a tree of life."
Proverb 13:12

Jerilyn walked the two blocks and encountered a quaint, beautiful little town. A huge, decorated Christmas tree graced the space in the middle of the square near the Simpson County Courthouse building. Holly wreaths adorned the doors of the businesses. She looked to her left on South Main Street and noticed the marquis for the Roxy Theatre. The film *Citizen Kane* would be shown twice daily at twelve-thirty and seven-thirty, except on Saturday when *Dumbo* was presented at nine in the morning and again at noon and three o'clock.

She didn't feel ready to enter the hotel, so she walked around the square and saw two churches, each with a beautiful manger scene outside their doors. People milled around, going in and out of the stores. She read the signs: *Gillespie Dry Goods, Massey's Furniture, Hughes Hardware, Mallory*

Jewelry, and *Blue Rose Bakery* were among the many businesses. Finally, Jerilyn meandered towards Christmas Hotel, not looking forward to asking for assistance. She sat on a bench in the park, directly across the street from the hotel. For the first time, she opened and read the note to Captain and Mrs. Bazell from Mr. Blakely, in which he explained her situation.

She looked up and scrutinized the hotel. The brick building was quite old, but well-kept. It was five stories tall and built in the Italianate style architecture, which was uncommon in the South, but highly prevalent in Dayton and most of the Northern cities. A massive stone block near the top of the fifth story bore the deep carving CHRISTMAS HOTEL. Just below this she could see another carving, also in stone: WHERE JESUS' BIRTH IS A DAILY CELEBRATION.

The massive double glass doors, two stories high, were recessed about twenty inches into the building. Two angels, carved into the façade adjacent to each brass trimmed door, gave an unusual but very welcoming feature. Below the right hand angel, a brass plaque was inscribed with the date 1850. Gas coach lights shone in welcome above both angels.

Jerilyn's eyes traveled the building façade, beginning at the four narrow two-story windows on each side of the double doors, up to the third, fourth and fifth floors, to several high narrow windows, along with two balconies on each of the three floors.

A clock in the square rooftop cupola faced the park. From where she sat, she could see at least six chimney tops on the roof, inside the balustrade surrounding the top of the building. That completed the front of the building. The side of the building on East Cedar Street appeared to be solid brick, except for the windows and balconies that began on the third floor and continued up to the fifth floor. *It reminds me of the Victory Theatre in Dayton. Both are such magnificent buildings.*

Well, it's now or never. She realized she was wasting time and putting off the inevitable. She sighed, grabbed the handle of her suitcase, and stood. After a deep breath, she squared her shoulders, stood tall, and marched across the street. She opened one of the heavy, brass-handled double doors to the lobby and stepped inside, then turned in awe as the door slowly closed behind her. The highly polished floors contained checkered squares of black and white marble, but the two-storied lobby's focal point was a horseshoe shaped curved grand staircase leading to the second floor. Holly and cranberries wrapped the beautifully hand-carved cherry banister.

In the middle of the horseshoe of the staircase, a life-size model of the manger scene stood. Mary, Joseph, the shepherd men, all gazed upon the small babe in the manger. Life-size statutes of the barn animals and the three wise men finished the Nativity background. The compelling scene transported her back nearly two thousand years to the birth of the baby Jesus.

On the floor in the middle of the room, a Christmas tree nearly touched the ceiling to the second floor. Was it real or artificial? As she took in the magnificence of the tree and the beautiful ornaments, she lifted her chin and saw the angel atop the tree, seemingly smiling down on her in greeting. She walked to the tree for a closer examination. Touching a branch, Jerilyn nodded and smiled. It was indeed artificial; one of the popular goose feather trees, and obviously specially made. She had never known of one so large.

The plush furniture in the lobby appeared comfortable and inviting. Several sofas, high back chairs, and cherry end tables decorated the room, with beautiful oriental rugs in the middle of the groupings. Along the Cedar Street wall a fire roared in a stone fireplace. The hearth was at least seven feet wide, and a mantle about six feet above the fireplace opening held four stockings with names on each one. In her opinion, the lobby was tasteful, not garish. She could picture herself curled up in one of the chairs in front of the fireplace, and reading one of the books she'd brought with her; *The Song of Bernadette* by Franz Werfel.

She walked forward for a closer look, for surely no one would mind her reading the names on the stockings that were on view to guests. One was Captain Bazell, another Mary Bazell, a third said Christopher, and the fourth was for Lily. She wondered who Christopher and Lily were. Were they the children of the Bazells, or a husband and wife who worked at Christmas Hotel?

Along the wall off to the side of the room, behind a long lobby desk, she noticed for the first time an elderly couple sitting on high stools, watching her while she observed the room. Feeling embarrassed, she turned and walked toward them. To her young eyes, the couple looked to be quite elderly; and both were stylishly dressed in attire from the nineteenth century. They smiled in welcome as she approached the huge old cherry desk. Jerilyn noticed sixty numbered pigeonholes on the table behind them for the mail and messages for the guests.

The old gentleman stood as she approached the desk. "Good afternoon, young lady. Welcome to Christmas Hotel!" he said with enthusiasm.

The old lady said nothing, but continued to

smile warmly.

"Good afternoon to you, too," responded Jerilyn, with as much zeal as she could muster under the circumstances. She was not prone to asking for hand-outs, but she approached the subject with honesty. "I have a note from Mr. Jonathan Blakely at the diner in the train station," she said tentatively, as she handed him the note.

The old gentlemen adjusted his glasses and read. When he had finished, he passed the note to the woman.

In haste, Jerilyn blurted, "I'm not begging for provisions. I'll do whatever work you need done to pay for my room and board. Mr. Blakely offered me a job, too, so as soon as I'm able, I'll move on and continue my course to Nashville. I won't be a charity case for you."

At that, the old lady spoke for the first time. "I think that introductions are in order," she said softly. "This is my husband, Captain Jacob Barnabas Bazell, and I am Mary Eve Winters Bazell. According to the note, you are Jerilyn Seifert, and an unfortunate occurrence has separated you from your purse. You are not the first person who has suffered misfortune and was sent to us by Mr. Blakely. You will probably not be the last. As long as evil exists, these things will happen. You will not be treated as a charity case at

Christmas Hotel."

Captain Bazell smiled, and then continued for his wife. "We will offer you a fair share of work for your room and board, and if you choose to work at the diner for Mr. Blakely, I know he will pay you a reasonable wage for the hours you work."

Mrs. Bazell added, "Furthermore, you are so pretty that I'm certain you will be given worthy tips." Jerilyn could see a twinkle in her faded blue eyes.

Jerilyn blushed, and the anxiety she had felt began to subside. "Thank you so much. I promise to work competently, and I will not be a burden to you."

A young man entered the lobby from a back room that most likely was the hotel's office. Captain Bazell made the introduction. "Miss Jerilyn Seifert, I would like you to meet Mr. Christopher Wright. He manages Christmas Hotel for us. As you can perhaps tell, my wife and I are a little up in years, so we are mostly figureheads here, but we still enjoy greeting each and every guest."

Mr. Wright shook Jerilyn's hand amiably, and smiled. "I'm pleased to meet you, Miss Seifert."

"Actually it's Mrs. Seifert. However, I'm a widow." The words sounded strange to her. She had not yet admitted this new status to strangers. "My husband was in the navy medical unit at Pearl

Harbor. He was killed aboard his ship."

"You have my sincere condolences, Mrs. Seifert," Mr. Wright said, with obvious sincerity.

Mr. Wright then turned to the Bazells. "I must remind you I filled the last available room an hour before Mrs. Seifert arrived. I'm afraid we have all the rooms booked until after New Year's Day."

With one finger, Captain Bazell tapped his cheek and closed his eyes, obviously in deep thought. Finally, he turned to his wife and spoke softly to her. "Let's go into the office and discuss this matter," He turned to Mr. Wright and Jerilyn. "We will be right back. Mrs. Seifert, please have a seat on one of the chairs in the lobby."

Mr. Wright took a seat behind the check-in desk, and Jerilyn picked up her suitcase and walked to the chair as instructed. At this moment she felt over anxious, guessing that her fate was in the hands of Captain and Mrs. Bazell. She could hear her parents' voices ringing in her ears: *Pray to the Lord in all situations.* That was easier said than done. She couldn't even remember the last time she had prayed. She couldn't imagine God listening to her after all this time anyway.

After what seemed an hour, but was probably only a few minutes, the Bazells made their way to her, heavily leaning on their canes, and took their seats on one of the sofas.

"Christopher, would you please come here and sit with us for a moment?" Captain Bazell asked.

Mr. Wright stepped from behind the desk and took a seat near them. Jerilyn could not help watching a young couple walking down the grand staircase, hand-in-hand. They acted like newlyweds, gazing at each other, exactly as she and Ken had just two years earlier when they were first married.

Captain Bazell waited until the young couple departed the hotel before he began again. "We do have one room available." He looked to his wife, obviously for confirmation, who nodded her head with approval. "As I was saying, there is a room available you may use. It is room number seven."

At that, Mr. Wright jerked his head from Mrs. Bazell back to Captain Bazell. "But–" he started to say.

However, Captain Bazell cut him off, waving his hand. "It's all right, Christopher. Mrs. Bazell and I are in complete agreement. We want Mrs. Seifert to use the room, as long as she will reside with us."

Wide-eyed, and slack-jawed, Mr. Wright looked from Mr. Bazell to Mrs. Bazell as though he could not believe what he was hearing. "Room number seven?" he questioned quietly, but loudly enough for Jerilyn to overhear.

Mr. Bazell smiled. "Yes, we are offering it to

Mrs. Seifert."

Mrs. Bazell turned to Jerilyn. "It is a very special room that has not been used in some time," she explained. "It is our wish that it is only entered once a week to be dusted. Even the furnishings have never been changed. The room looks as it did the day the hotel opened in 1850. It is the only room of the sixty that has never been updated. Captain Bazell and I hope you will find the room comfortable, and that you will enjoy your stay with us."

Jerilyn waited for a fuller explanation of this peculiar room, but it appeared the Bazells had said enough. However, her interest was piqued. Jerilyn always enjoyed a good mystery. She was currently reading Agatha Christie's mystery, *Evil Under the Sun*; at least she'd started reading it before Ken died.

Captain Bazell continued, "Mrs. Seifert, dinner is served at six o'clock." He pointed in the direction of the hotel's dining room. "Please join us at our table tonight, and we will go over your duties. If you work at the diner in the train station for Jonathan Blakely, we will make certain your duties do not overlap. Christopher, after you help Mrs. Seifert settle into her room, please accompany her around the hotel for a guided tour to prepare her for her work with us."

The Bazells rose to signify the discussion was over. They made their way back to the desk, each heavily relying on their canes for support.

Mr. Wright and Jerilyn stood, and he picked up her suitcase. He regarded Jerilyn and she knew what he was thinking. It was as if she could read his mind that the suitcase was not very heavy, so what was she doing traveling with so little? He said nothing as he led the way up the beautiful staircase with Jerilyn close behind. They walked down the hallway and stopped at room #7.

Mr. Wright reached in his pocket and pulled out a huge ring of keys. He looked through the keys until he found one engraved with the number seven. He opened the door and motioned for Jerilyn to enter first. A step behind her, Mr. Wright entered the room and lit the kerosene lamp on the nightstand. She could only gasp in awe. "Wow, have we entered another time?

His dimples danced when he grinned at her in amusement. Her eyes were drawn to the high four-poster oak bed with a sheer curtain wrapped around it and a marble top oak dresser which held an attached matching oak framed mirror. A lady's vanity sat next to the dresser. It held a silver tray on which lay a mother of pearl hairbrush, comb, and hand mirror. Two brocade chairs with a table between them and with a very old kerosene lamp atop the table sat in front of one of the windows. Heavy deep green velvet drapes pooled on the floor from four floor-to-ceiling windows. In the middle of the four windows, french doors led to a small balcony.

"You're in one of the two special rooms overlooking the square on North Main Street. From this vantage point you can look down on the square, see all the Christmas decorations, the townspeople milling around the square, and the numerous decorated businesses."

He showed Jerilyn how the windows and french doors opened and locked. Together, they stepped out upon the balcony, and the young couple who had earlier walked down the grand staircase of the hotel, now walked hand-in-hand on the sidewalk of the square. They then snuggled together on the same bench on which she had sat earlier; still holding hands. She realized she was staring, and turned and stepped back into the room.

Mr. Wright locked the doors and closed the drapes.

A beautiful antique writing desk with very small drawers and pigeon holes stood against another wall. Beside a large armoire, she stared at a closed door. She was aware that Mr. Wright was watching her, and he opened the door.

"This is what they called a water closet in the

nineteenth century," he explained.

Jerilyn looked in and saw it contained a toilet with a pull chain, and beside that, a sink with a mirror overhead. A divider separated the toilet from a small shower stall.

"All the rooms still have the water closet, which helps generate the character of Christmas Hotel," continued Mr. Wright. "People come from many states around Kentucky to enjoy the ambiance here. Weddings have been performed here in our chapel, especially at Christmas. You'll see the chapel when we do the tour.

"I am instructed to give you the guided tour of the hotel, and you are to sit with the Bazells for dinner," he stated in a matter of fact way as he checked his watch. "It is now two o'clock. I suggest you unpack and rest. I can return, at say, around four-thirty. That will give us plenty of time for the tour, and still have you at dinner by six o'clock. How does that sound?"

"It sounds just fine with me."

"I'll give you your own room key when I return." He closed the door and left Jerilyn with her thoughts.

No husband. No money. Alone in a strange town. What have I done?

Chapter Three

Questions

"Because to every purpose there is time and judgment, therefore the misery of man is great upon him."
Ecclesiastes 8:6

Late Monday afternoon
December 15, 1941
Jerilyn had plenty of time to wash her face, unpack, and take a brief nap before the tour at four-thirty. When she awoke, she dressed in her good navy blue suit, opened the drapes to a setting sun, and sat in one of the chairs by the windows to await Mr. Wright. She turned in her chair to watch the people down on the square, hurrying to and fro to make their purchases.

The young manager arrived to fetch her promptly at four-thirty. When she opened the door to his knock, she saw he too was dressed for dinner, looking impeccable in his dark blue suit. She had not taken the time to notice him before, but now she took in his newly shaved face, clean fresh smell, and his neatly combed dark brown wavy hair. When he handed her the room key as promised, she also observed his neatly trimmed and clean fingernails.

"Let's begin on the fifth floor and make our way down. Are you up for all the steps? We have a small lift, if that will suit you better."

"No, I'm fine with the stairs."

When they reached the top floor, the fifth floor, Mr. Wright pulled the brass handles, one at a time, to two large oak doors with C engraved into one and H for the other. He used the wall hooks to hold each door open to reveal a ballroom with a wide plank southern pine floor, polished to perfection, and six elegant crystal chandeliers attached to the ceiling across its length. Plush green velvet high back chairs lined the walls. Jerilyn had heard about ballrooms in stylish hotels, but this was her first experience seeing one.

"This is an antebellum hotel, built in 1850 prior to the Civil War, thus the word antebellum. It was built by a prominent Christian family in the community: the Thomas Hoy family. The family's intentions were for all that stayed here, no matter what season of the year, to find their Christmas miracle. They hoped each person would experience the love of our Lord Jesus. They wanted all to see that the miracle of Christmas was all year around, not just on the celebrated birth of Jesus. That is why they named it Christmas Hotel."

Jerilyn listened to his words, but felt the Lord had forgotten her, just as she had forgotten Him. She did not expect any miracle here – or anywhere. How could the Lord possibly care about her? She had not taken the time to spend even a moment with Him in years. She couldn't remember the last time she read her Bible or prayed. She didn't pack it when she left home. At her Dayton home, it lay open on display on her coffee table, gathering dust. She had only packed what she considered her bare essentials, and only items she considered of importance. The Bible was not one of those essentials.

Mr. Wright closed the ballroom doors, and she followed him down to the fourth floor. As they walked, Mr. Wright continued his narrative. "Notice the artwork as you walk through the halls of each floor. Each picture is labeled for the year, who or what the picture is regarding, along with the photographer or artist. You'll find more portraits of the previous owners and their children throughout these floors. You'll also find paintings of our town square in each decade since the hotel's inception. All the business spaces have changed ownership throughout the years except the corner where Christmas Hotel stands."

Unlocking the door to one of the guest rooms, he continued his well-rehearsed speech. "All fifty-nine rooms on the second, third and fourth floors are identical, and are decorated in a twentieth century up-to-date fashion, unlike your room that is still bedecked in the nineteenth century. However, each room still has the small, original water closet attached to the room, along with the shower stall. Each of the guest rooms is larger than a room in an average sized hotel. In addition, long before the Gideon's began placing Bibles in hotel rooms over thirty years ago, this hotel had a King James Bible placed in all sixty rooms, the chapel, and the lobby, from its inception."

Jerilyn glanced at the young manager, saying nothing, but she was still puzzled by Mr. and Mrs. Bazell's story about her room not being used in some time. Why would a perfectly good room like hers not be let to a guest? Why was it never updated as the others were?

"Do you have any questions or comments, Mrs. Seifert?"

She plucked up courage to ask. "I have only two thoughts that baffle me, Mr. Wright. One is, why does my room have a Victorian décor, but the other fifty-nine rooms are much more modern? Also, why is my room never let?"

He did not hesitant with his answer. In a stoic

expression, he answered. “I think I will allow Captain and Mrs. Bazell to answer those questions for you.” At that, he turned, continued at a brisk pace, and she hurried along behind him.

Jerilyn grew even more puzzled, and a bit miffed by his quick and evasive answer, but gritted her teeth, and said nothing. She continued to follow the Mr. Wright in silence. When they reached the main floor, he walked with her through the lobby and into the hotel’s dining room. Mr. Wright continued with his speech. “This room, like the ballroom, contains six elegant crystal chandeliers. You’ll notice tables for two or four persons fill the room, all draped with crisp white linen tablecloths and matching napkins. In the corner of each tablecloth and napkin the monogram CH has been embroidered, and a red runner lay across the middle of the tables, with a holly and cranberry centerpiece. The ornate silverware was also engraved with CH. This dining room has been decorated similarly since Christmas Hotel opened in 1850. We know this because the Hoys kept meticulous records. Most of this silverware is the original pieces from 1850. A silverware company has matched the pieces and keeps us supplied as needed.”

Christopher pointed out the glasses. “Note each glass is embossed with a replica of the hotel and the letters CH.

He swept his hand in another direction. “Do you see the floor-to-ceiling windows overlooking the hotel’s courtyard?” Jerilyn followed his gaze and nodded. “Observe the two french doors leading to the courtyard and the red velvet drapes pooling on the floor. In the nineteenth century, extra-long drapes were a sign of wealth. In the summer, out in the courtyard, tables are set up around the decorated pine tree for those wishing to dine outside. I realize many of our Christmas guests have not visited in the summer, but the courtyard contains manicured flowerbeds and hanging potted plants with roses trailing from the pergola and trellises. It’s quite beautiful.”

He pointed in the opposite direction. “The corner fireplace is used in the winter, and as you see, our detailed staff has a roaring fire set.” He chuckled, displaying his dimples again. “They also clean the ashes each morning. “Maybe he does have a sense of humor, and he’s not so stiff and formal all the time, Jerilyn thought.

Two men polished the silver until it gleamed, while two other men set crystal glasses on the tables. Jerilyn had never experienced anything so chic in her life. The room exuded elegance in every detail.

The third exit from the dining room led into the

modern kitchen. Gleaming copper pots and pans hung on ceiling hooks, and ten men were busy preparing the evening meal for the guests. The chef and his nine assistants paused while the manager introduced them to Jerilyn. They smiled unpretentiously as Mr. Wright introduced them as the best cooks in Simpson County.

Including the dining room door, six other doors led from the kitchen. Mr. Wright proceeded to show where the other five doors led. Opening the first door, Jerilyn observed the large well stocked pantry. The second door was to the supply room for the housekeeping staff. The third door opened to a staff break room, and the fourth door led to the courtyard. The fifth door led to the basement steps. The manager turned on the light, and Jerilyn followed him down.

The housekeepers washed the hotel linens in one area, and Jerilyn could see a storage area for the hotel in another. Along one wall she counted five electric clothes washers, and along an adjacent wall, five electric clothes dryers. She smiled wryly. At her Dayton home she still used the old wringer washer, and hung her clothes on a line in the backyard to dry on sunny days, and in her basement in the winter or on rainy days.

She noticed a locked, fenced-in area containing several crates marked CEB. She was curious, but decided not to appear prying by asking Mr. Wright about the crates, remembering his other elusive answers. They climbed back up the steps, and passed through the kitchen into the lobby.

"I have only one other room to show you," Mr. Wright said.

They walked across the lobby. He opened the arched door and Jerilyn stepped in. It was the chapel, and straight ahead on the wall behind the pulpit, hung a large wooden cross. One main aisle split the room, with six pews on each side. "This is where the small weddings are held," Mr. Wright said reverently. "Numerous guests and the townspeople come here to pray, and over the years many have found the answer to their prayers."

I think it will take more than this chapel to find the answer to my prayers, Jerilyn thought with disparagement.

The manager looked at his watch. "Well, it appears as though our time is up. I need to return you to the dining room. Captain and Mrs. Bazell are very prompt. I wouldn't want you to be late on my account."

"Will you be joining us?" asked Jerilyn.

"No, I need to head home. Someone is expecting me." He closed the chapel door and they walked to the dining room while they talked. "You will find the Bazells at their table overlooking the courtyard.

Good evening, Mrs. Seifert. I will be at the front desk at seven o'clock tomorrow morning if you have further questions."

At that, he turned and briskly walked away from her. Many questions arose. Someone was expecting him. His stocking, along with one for someone named Lily, was hanging over the fireplace. Was Lily his wife? Why was her room, room #7, still in Victorian décor and not used in many years – until today? Why were the crates in the basement marked CEB? The mysteries and the secrecy began to intrigue her.

Other guests now descended the stairs. *I suppose I should just look at this as a new adventure in my life, until I have enough money to continue on to Nashville. At least I now have a roof over my head, and food. Tomorrow morning, if Mr. Blakely hires me at his diner, I will also have some money. Things definitely look better than they did earlier.*

She entered the dining room and headed to the Bazells' table.

Chapter Four

A New Adventure

"In every thing give thanks: for this is the will of God in Christ Jesus concerning you."
1 Thessalonians 5:18

Tuesday morning
December 16, 1941
The night before at dinner, the Bazells had discussed her duties. They suggested Jerilyn would be a lovely hostess for their dining room, during the supper hour, greeting and seating the guests. If she worked for Mr. Blakely at his diner in the train station, they would coordinate their schedule for Jerilyn with his.

Jerilyn was up at five o'clock that morning and arrived at Jonathan Blakely's diner by six.

Nettie Sue greeted her. "Mr. Blakely is in his office and expecting you. You can go on back."

Jerilyn walked behind the counter and tapped on the door.

"Come in," a pleasant voice invited.

She stepped into the small, but sufficient room.

Mr. Blakely sat behind the desk, but stood when she entered. He motioned for her to have a seat on the other side of his desk. He asked her about her work experience, which she explained had only been in an office at a factory in Dayton, Ohio. The name of the company was National Cash Register.

"I know all about National Cash Register, or NCR for short. The cash register I use out front had been built by the famous Dayton company.

"I really have no work for an office girl, but if you're willing, Nettie Sue will train you to wait on guests in the diner. I would need you to work breakfast and lunch. I have plenty of help during dinner. I will supply two uniforms. Nettie Sue will find them for you in the appropriate size, and you can embroider your name on them. You will make better tips if the guests know your name. You can begin now if you like. Tomorrow morning you would need to be here by six, and your shift will end by two o'clock. You won't be needed on Saturday. That's when my teenage niece works, and of course we're closed on Sunday. Nettie Sue opens at five o'clock and she can handle the counter until you arrive. We get diners from off the train, but many of the townspeople come in, too. I will pay you ten dollars per week, plus you will make tips. Nettie Sue says she makes about three dollars every day from tips. So, are you interested?"

"Yes, sir, I would be pleased to work for you. I'll do my best to learn the job as quickly as possible."

He rose and walked to the door. "Nettie Sue, if you have a minute would you please get–" He turned quickly. "May I call you Jerilyn?"

"Yes, please do."

He turned back to Nettie Sue. "Please find Jerilyn two uniforms, and I'll watch your counter while you help her."

Jerilyn followed Nettie Sue into the locker room. Nettie Sue found the right size uniforms, both pale blue, and helped Jerilyn with her white starched apron and little white waitress cap.

"What shall I do today?" asked Jerilyn.

"Just follow me for a while. While I'm serving the guests, I can show you where to find things. When I feel you're ready, I'll give you some customers. It's a large counter with thirty stools."

"Have you been working here alone?" Jerilyn asked in wonder, overcome by the thought of such a busy day.

Nettie Sue laughed. "Only for ten days. The other girl working with me left to get married. Mr. Blakely has been trying to replace her. Booker, my fiancé, says I'm working too hard. You certainly arrived at the right time."

"I hope I'll be able to do this," Jerilyn responded nervously, noticing Nettie Sue's engagement ring for the first time. The thought of fiancés and marriage was too painful to discuss with someone who was nearly a stranger.

Nettie Sue patted Jerilyn's arm. "I'm sure you'll be just fine. Try not to worry."

Jerilyn dressed in one of the uniforms, and they returned to the counter, and Mr. Blakely returned to his office. It was only six-thirty, but there were now five people at the stools. Mr. Wright, the hotel manager, sat at one stool with a cute little girl around five-years-old.

Jerilyn walked over and greeted him. "Good morning, Mr. Wright. I suppose I didn't expect to see you here."

"Good morning, Mrs. Seifert. I come here most mornings with my daughter Lily before work. We try to have at least two meals together each day. For supper, we eat at home or at Christmas Hotel. This is our time together ... right, sweetheart?"

He hugged the little girl to him while he talked. So Lily was *not* Mr. Wright's wife. She was a small child, very pretty with little brown curls all over her head and big brown eyes. She reminded Jerilyn of Shirley Temple, down to the dimpled cheeks.

Lily giggled when she answered her father. "Yes. My daddy and I are always together, except of course when he's at work." She smiled up at Jerilyn, showing her missing front teeth.

Jerilyn noticed Mr. Wright's coffee cup was empty. "May I get you some more coffee?"

He glanced at his watch. "I should have time for a half a cup."

Jerilyn turned around, spotted the coffee pot and poured him his coffee. She looked to Lily. "May I get you anything else, Lily?"

"No, thank you. I'm fine." Lily looked up to her father and asked with the honesty of a child, "She's pretty, isn't she, Daddy?"

Jerilyn and Mr. Wright looked at each other in surprise, but Jerilyn quickly looked away, embarrassed by the innocence of the child's question.

However, Mr. Wright responded to his daughter. "Yes, she is. Although, *we* need to get moving or Daddy will be late for work." He jumped up and threw on his coat, grabbed Lily's coat, put it on her, and buttoned it. Lily pulled on her mittens while her father adjusted her hat and scarf. He grabbed his own hat, holding it respectfully in his hand. "Good day, Mrs. Seifert. I'll see you later at Christmas Hotel."

Lily waved to Jerilyn and Jerilyn waved back, as they hurried out the door.

****

Jerilyn was off at two o'clock and extremely tired after her first day at Mr. Blakely's diner, although it was a good feeling. She had quickly learned her way around the diner, and Nettie Sue had given her half the stools by lunchtime, and she made seventy-five cents in tips. She arrived back at the hotel, waved to Captain and Mrs. Bazell at the desk, didn't see Mr. Wright, and hurried to her room where she took a quick shower and lay down on the bed for a short nap.

After a well-deserved rest she rose and searched through her meager amount of clothes for a proper dress. She had two dresses which would probably be suitable for the hotel dining room. One was black and the other was a pale blue to match her eyes.

She examined her face in the mirror, and realized she needed some powder and a touch of rouge. Her cheeks appeared somewhat hollow and pale. She twisted her shoulder-length dark brown wavy hair into a chignon at the nape of her neck, and pinned it with two mother of pearl and brass hinged combs, the only ornamental items she had brought with her, outside of her wedding band. She realized she had probably lost about five pounds since the telegram.

She touched her stomach. Presently, her pregnancy did not show, but she knew that would not last much longer. She wondered how her supervisors at her new jobs would take the news. At least the morning sickness was over, but would she be able to work up until the baby was born? She would need to put back some money for the needed layette, if she kept the baby. She had serious thoughts about giving the baby up for adoption. A child needed a mother *and* a father.

At five o'clock she was in the dining room and ready for her instructions. Mr. Wright was there to show her where things were kept, and how to check the tables to ensure they were set properly. With one glance he surveyed the room, noting one table missing a salad fork and another table missing a water glass.

He showed Jerilyn where to find them, and added his instructions on seating the guests. "I will be here by your side for this first evening, Mrs. Seifert, and then tomorrow you should be able to handle it alone."

"Thank you." She cocked her head, sizing him up, and then smiled. "Since we will be working together, may we dispense with the formalities? Would you please call me Jerilyn?"

He smiled back. "I will, but only if you will call me Christopher."

"Request granted Mr.–, I mean Christopher."

The Bazells arrived promptly at five fifty-five that evening and Jerilyn greeted them, while Christopher pulled out Mrs. Bazell's chair to seat her. By six-thirty all the hotel's guests and several of the townspeople had arrived for supper. The waiters served them, and Christopher taught Jerilyn how to oversee the room to make sure things ran smoothly. It would be her duty to walk the floor, and make certain every guest was content. If they had need of more coffee, tea, water, etcetera, she would aid the waiters.

The dining room closed at eight o'clock, but Christopher had provided her with a list of her close-out duties. He would observe her close-out tonight, and be available if she had questions. It was necessary to help prepare the dining room for breakfast. The linens needed stripping, taken to the laundry area in the basement, and fresh linens returned to the tables. The crystal and silverware were washed in the kitchen. The silver would be polished by other staff before the next meal. It would be Jerilyn's duties, as hostess, to supervise the set-up of the dining room.

At eight-thirty the room was complete, and Jerilyn's feet were hurting. She just wanted to head to her room and rest. This was to be her schedule five days a week. Thankfully, she would be off on Saturday and Sunday from both jobs.

"Jerilyn, you are a natural," complimented Christopher. "I don't believe the Bazells could have found a better hostess for the dining room. I've been standing in as the host for most of the past month until the position was filled. I must say that with my management duties, this role was becoming too much for me, and I've been missing my time with my daughter Lily. I thank God you arrived on our doorstep. Although, you arrived here because of an unfortunate incident, you are definitely an answer to my prayers, *and* a blessing."

Overwhelmed with the praise, Jerilyn blushed. "Thank you, Christopher, for the encouragement. I will do my best to make you and the Bazells proud of me. I don't know about being an answer to prayer or a blessing, but I thank you for the approval. I know you are anxious to get home to Lily. Please tell her sweet dreams for me."

"I will, Jerilyn. We'll see you in the morning down at the station diner, and we'll make sure we sit on your side."

Chapter Five

Revelations

"My soul melteth for heaviness: strengthen thou me according unto thy word."
Psalm 119:28

"Then they cry unto the Lord in their trouble, and he saveth them out of their distresses."
Psalm 107:19

Late Tuesday evening
December 16, 1941
Exhausted, Jerilyn climbed the staircase to her room, took the key from her pocket, and opened the door. Once inside, she turned the lock and tossed the key onto the desk, walked to the french doors, opened them, and stepped into the night on the balcony. She breathed in the fresh air and slowly exhaled. It was a cold December evening, but the view was beautiful with all the lit trees in the park inside the square, along with the large decorated Christmas tree in front of the Simpson County Courthouse. The town still had gas lights, giving it

the appearance of a quaint nineteenth century village. Her thoughts turned to Ken. *He would love this charming town. The people are warm and friendly. I wonder if he was ever here, given the close proximity to Nashville. This would have been a wonderful place for our honeymoon.*

"Ken, can you hear me?" she said aloud. "I wish you were here with me. Do you know how much I miss you?

"Oh, I'm being silly. Of course he can't hear me ... but I wish he could. Now I'm even talking to myself! God, You can tell Ken I love him. Would You?" She let out a huge sigh. "Now I'm even talking to God, and He doesn't care about me."

She decided it was time to write her parents and let them know she was well, and had not one, but two jobs. She surmised they would be worried if they knew she'd not arrived in Nashville, and she wanted them to know about the beautiful Christmas Hotel and that she was not living in some seedy establishment.

She closed and locked the french doors, drew the drapes, and sat down at the desk to look for writing paper and a pen. The pigeon holes were empty, so she opened each of the three small drawers. The first two drawers were also empty.

She tried the third drawer, but it was stiff to pull. This drawer was different from the other two.

There was a spring along one side of the drawer. When she pulled the spring, the bottom of the drawer slid backwards into the rear of the desk, leaving a secret space underneath. The drawer contained a false bottom! In it she could see a small book. She picked it up and opened it to the first page. It was a very old diary in a dark brown cracked leather cover, dated 1883 by Carrie Emeline. It was fifty-eight years old! Jerilyn's heart quickened with excitement. Taking great care, she gently opened the yellowed pages of the diary and began to read.

Much of January through March spoke of events with Carrie Emeline's betrothed, Seth Johnson. Carrie Emeline wrote about life in general in the small community of Rock Camp in south western Ohio. She spoke of going to church, ice skating, and sleigh rides with friends in the winter.

Jerilyn settled down for a long read, and discovered Carrie Emeline was her parents' only child, and she loved them so much, and they loved her. She was active in her church, teaching the children under age ten in her Sunday school class. She discussed salvation with the children and gave them her own testimony. She told of how she had come under conviction at the age of eleven, when she realized she needed Jesus Christ. She asked Him to come in to her heart, and the love of Jesus filled her soul. She prayed daily for "her" children.

Jerilyn thought back to the day she had done the same, when she also was eleven. However, she strayed from the Lord, and it appeared Carrie Emeline had not.

On April 14, 1883, Carrie Emeline wrote: *Today is my twenty-first birthday. Seth is escorting me to the church social tonight. I'm so excited! My parents bought me a new dress to wear; my first dress with a stylish bustle.*

On April 17 Carrie Emeline wrote: *Seth has not been able to find work. He heard about extra workers needed for the Northern Pacific Railroad that will connect the Northwestern states to the Northeastern states. The article states that if they have enough workers, they can complete the nineteen-year-project by the end of this year. Seth said this will give us enough money to marry on Christmas Eve this year, as planned. He leaves tomorrow and I will miss him; however, I recognize that he is working to procure our future.*

From April through September, Carrie Emeline continued to write about the daily events and activities, such as swimming in the pond in the summer, and canning vegetables from the harvest in September. Then on September 23, 1883 she wrote: *How will I live? What shall I do? God has abandoned me. He has allowed the death of my beloved Seth. According to the letter from Seth's supervisor, Seth and two other men were injured while coupling two railroad cars. Seth is dead!*

Jerilyn noted similar writings of deep sadness and despair throughout the remainder of September.

On October 3, 1883 Carrie Emeline wrote: *Today the body of Seth was returned home and buried. I planted chrysanthemums on the mound of earth where his body lies. Dear God ... why?*

"I know just how she feels," Jerilyn said aloud. "Although *she* had a grave to visit. I don't know where Ken's body is ... and most likely never will."

On October 4, 1883 Carrie Emeline wrote: *Another dreary day. I am so depressed. My friends came by to cheer me up. I told my mother I did not wish to see them.*

On October 5, 1883 Carrie Emeline wrote: *My life is miserable. Why, God, am I still allowed to live? My heart died with Seth.*

Throughout October and November the writings didn't change.

On November 30, 1883 Carrie Emeline wrote: *I have just read Psalm 69:1-3. Save me, O God; for the waters are come in unto my soul; I sink in deep mire, where there is no standing: I am come into deep waters, where the floods overflow me. I am weary of my crying: my throat is dried: mine eyes fail while I wait for my God.*

Jerilyn sat back holding the diary to her breast and a single tear fell on her cheek. *That is exactly how I feel. I cannot endure life without my beloved Ken.*

Jerilyn could certainly identify with Carrie Emeline's feelings here, and she felt a flood of hot tears on her cheeks – tears of anger directed toward God. She roughly wiped them away in rage, but continued to read.

Then on December 1, 1883 Carrie Emeline's parents made a decision. Carrie Emeline wrote: *My parents are taking me away. They say I need to look at new surroundings. I do not know about that decision. They heard about a hotel in Franklin, Kentucky called Christmas Hotel. I really do not even desire to think about Christmas. Seth and I would have married on Christmas Eve. Now he is gone. I really do not see how this vacation will do me any good. They should leave me here and go alone. They certainly do not need me to spoil their life.*

On December 3, 1883 Carrie Emeline wrote: *We are packed and leaving. I just found out that this is a 300 mile journey! Did my parents think that we really needed to go that far for a change of scenery? Evidently, my aunt and uncle in West Virginia have been to Christmas Hotel, and gave a glowing report on the hotel and the village of Franklin, Kentucky. Therefore, that's where my parents want to go. Father says that it will be a wonderful experience returning to one of the Southern states. Our country is healing, since the time he served as a Union Captain in the Civil War, and he wants us to do our part to promote the healing. Our neighbors are taking us and all our trunks to the train station in Huntington, West Virginia. From there we will take the train to Frankfort, the capital city of Kentucky. Then we will continue on to Elizabethtown, Bowling Green, and finally Franklin, Kentucky. I hear it's only six miles from the Tennessee border. With all these trunks, I think my parents must have packed everything we own. I am beginning to wonder if my parents are ever planning to return to Rock Camp.*

Carrie Emeline wrote about what she saw on the journey. Much of what she saw was what Jerilyn remembered from her own train ride just a couple of days ago. Jerilyn whispered aloud, "I see my life paralleled with yours, Carrie Emeline. You and I are about the same age, and we both lost the men we loved. At least you don't have the added burden of worrying about the future of a baby."

On December 10, 1883 Carrie Emeline wrote: *The train is pulling into the station. Porters have gathered to load our trunks on the wagon. They will take us to Christmas Hotel. I am not sure what to expect.*

On December 11, 1883 Carrie Emeline wrote: *I must say the village is beautiful. There is a town square with a courthouse. All the gas lights around the square are lit. The trees in the park in the middle of the square are decorated with pine cones, fruit, and strung cranberries.*

She then described Christmas Hotel, and Jerilyn realized that even back in 1883 it looked very much as it had when she first saw it.

Carrie Emeline continued her description. *A giant tree stands proudly in the lobby, and decorated for a Victorian Christmas. It is loaded with fruit, nuts, pine cones, ribbon, and colored paper cut into strips and glued together in a chain. A glass angel perches atop the tree. The most amazing life-size nativity scene sits in the middle of the horseshoe shaped staircase, on the lobby floor.*

"I wonder if it was the same glass angel atop the tree and the same Nativity scene currently in the hotel," Jerilyn thought aloud.

Carrie Emeline wrote about the fireplace, staircase, and lobby, just as Jerilyn saw it. *We checked in at the front desk. Two rooms were assigned to us. My parents will be in room #8, and*

I will be beside them in room #7.

Jerilyn stopped reading and her heart beat faster. Thoughts began to fill her head. *Carrie Emeline's father was a Civil War captain, and Captain Bazell was probably a hundred years old ... or close to it. The crates in the basement marked CEB. Would that be Carrie Emeline Bazell? Christopher wouldn't answer my question about why the room was never let, but said I would need to speak to the Bazells. This room ... room #7 ... has not been used in years and was never redecorated. Was Carrie Emeline the last person to occupy it? Was that why Christopher appeared stunned that the Bazells allowed me to use it? Carrie Emeline wondered why so many trunks were brought. She even suspected her parents were moving here permanently. Is that what happened? Did they come here to purchase Christmas Hotel? If so ... what amazing love for their only child! To leave the life they knew for Carrie Emeline's happiness!*

Jerilyn checked her watch. It was now ten-thirty. She needed to get some sleep. Tomorrow would be a long day. The reading and the questions would have to wait, and so would the letter to her parents.

Chapter Six

A Time to Reflect

"Wherefore I desire that ye faint not at my tribulations for you, which is your glory."
Ephesians 3:13

Wednesday morning,
December 17, 1941
Jerilyn arrived at Mr. Blakely's diner in her uniform and ready for work at five fifty-five. Just as she was walking through the door she heard her name being called from the street. She turned and saw Christopher and Lily running to catch up.

"Good morning, Jerilyn," Christopher called, while holding Lily's hand.

Lily waved with her free hand and Jerilyn waved back, holding the door until they arrived. She walked through the diner, while Christopher removed Lily's and his outer garments, hanging them on the wall hooks. Jerilyn and Nettie Sue greeted each other, and Jerilyn deposited her coat in the locker room. She was behind the counter at six o'clock and ready to take orders.

Christopher and Lily sat on a stool and scanned the menu on the counter. Lily decided on French toast with a cup of hot chocolate. Christopher asked for sausage, two eggs over medium, toast, and coffee. Jerilyn called their order into the cook, poured Christopher's coffee, and made Lily's hot chocolate. So far they were the only two customers at her stools, while Nettie Sue had three stools in use.

Lily looked up at Jerilyn, and smiled happily. "Daddy came home late last night, Mrs. Seifert, but he still tucked me in and read me a story. He said he was helping you at Christmas Hotel. He said you learned really well." The precocious Lily rattled on while taking sips of her hot chocolate between each sentence. She now had a chocolate mustache. Christopher leaned over and used his napkin to dab at her upper lip.

Jerilyn thought her adorable. "Yes, your daddy was teaching me the skills needed as the dining room hostess. He's a very good teacher. I'm sorry you had to miss your dinner with your daddy. I know it's a special time for you."

"Yes, it is. Tonight Daddy said we can have dinner together at the hotel, but he won't be working."

"I see," said Jerilyn, raising one eyebrow and

looking pointedly at Christopher. “Maybe your daddy needs to see how well he taught his pupil.”

“Excuse me while I jump into this conversation,” Christopher said. “I hate to interrupt you ladies, but I’m certain my pupil has learned just fine.” He smiled at each of them.

Lily bounced right back into the conversation, but addressing Jerilyn. “I’m going to sing at church this Sunday. Will you come and hear me sing, Mrs. Seifert?”

Before Jerilyn could answer, the cook rang the bell twice, her signal that her food order was up. If he had rung once, it would have been Nettie Sue’s food. She excused herself to pick up the food at the pass-through window between the diner and the kitchen. Jerilyn rather hoped Lily had forgotten her question, not at all being interested in church.

Lily began to eat. Jerilyn had to admit she did have ladylike manners. Christopher had done a wonderful job raising her. Jerilyn remained curious about his wife.

They finished, paid the check, tipped Jerilyn well, and Christopher grabbed their coats from the wall hooks. Jerilyn knew Christopher had fifteen minutes to get to work. They both said goodbye to her, and said they would see her in the evening at dinner.

****

Jerilyn finished her shift at two o'clock, said goodbye to Nettie Sue and Mr. Blakely, and hurried over to the hotel. The sun did its best to brighten the cold afternoon. She entered the hotel, waved to Christopher and the Bazells, hurried up the staircase and entered her room, then threw her key on the desk. Just in case housekeeping came into her room, she had placed the diary back in the secret drawer. Retrieving it from the special place, she lay on the bed to read. She was anxious to discover more of the story even though she'd need to forego her nap.

On December 12, 1883 Carrie Emeline wrote: *I must admit the people are warm and caring. Thomas and Lucy Hoy own Christmas Hotel and have three daughters. The oldest is my age and her name is Sarah. The other two are Abigail: age 17, and Ella: age 14. They are going ice skating tomorrow at a pond near town and asked me to go with them. Reluctantly, I said I would.*

On December 13, 1883 Carrie Emeline wrote: *We went skating today. Several other young people were there, too. I met Sarah's fiancé. Although I felt somewhat melancholy, they were so happy that I could not begrudge their happiness. They were so kind to engage me in their social event.*

On December 14, 1883 Carrie Emeline wrote:

My parents had a secret meeting with Mr. and Mrs. Thomas Hoy. I wonder if my original suspicions about a permanent move here were true.

On December 15, 1883 Carrie Emeline wrote: *The Hoys invited my parents and me to attend church with them. I have not attended church since Seth died. I think it may be time to return.*

On Sunday, December 16, 1883 Carrie Emeline wrote: *The sermon today was on Isaiah 40:31. "But they that wait upon the Lord shall renew their strength; they shall mount up with wings as eagles; they shall run, and not be weary; and they shall walk, and not faint." I thank You, Lord, for that verse, as it has always been one of my favorites. I was so wrong when I thought You had forsaken me. I know You have always loved me. I'm sorry I lost faith in you. Please forgive me. I know that You loved Seth, even more than I did. I will not doubt why You took Seth home. I will not doubt Your will again. I will live the remainder of my days giving honor and glory to You. I seek Your forgiveness and I rededicate my life to You. A wise preacher once said to me, "To know Jesus, know hope; and no Jesus, no hope." He spelled know and no, so that I would understand. He was absolutely correct. I spent the remainder of the day crying out to the Lord and weeping tears of joy. I again felt close to Him.*

Jerilyn closed the diary. She bowed her head and began to cry out loud. *"Dear Lord, please help me. I need You. I can't do this alone."* She touched her stomach. *"Do you want me to give my baby up for adoption? A baby needs a father and a mother. Please let me know what I should do. I need hope, too. I'm sorry I have been distant for so long. I need Your help. If You still care about me, please help me. Please let me know that You are listening."*

She walked to her dresser, removed her last letter from Ken, and sat in a chair by the window to reread it.

5 December 1941
Dear Jerilyn,
Oh, my darling! I'm so happy we're going to be parents! I've already told every man I can find here on the ship in Pearl Harbor. The guys here are happy for us. The ones that are already fathers began showing me pictures of their children. Just think, next May I will be able to do the same. Do you want a boy or a girl? I don't really care. I wish I could be with you. Are you doing all right? Do you have any morning sickness? You take care and do what the doctor tells you.

I want you to know I've been having long talks with our chaplain. I know you were saved years ago. I really never understood salvation, and I never saw you attend church. You never seemed to think it was that important. Well, I just want to shout it to the walls – Jesus Christ saved my soul last week! The chaplain explained to me how everyone is a sinner. He showed me in the Bible that Jesus Christ died on the cross to pay our sin debt for us. He showed me where it says Christ rose from the grave and returned to heaven. I felt so convicted. I knew I needed Jesus Christ. I prayed with our chaplain, and I sensed the peace and assurance of Jesus Christ. The very next day he baptized me in the ocean. I hope you will go to church and rededicate your life to the Lord. I want us to raise our child with the knowledge of Jesus Christ. So, darling, I'm praying you will realize you need Jesus back in your life, for your sake and our child's.

I've known of men killed in the war, and although America is not officially involved, we may be soon. I hope I'm not killed, but if I am, I know the Bible says my spirit will return to the Father. I will be His child for eternity. I want that for our child, too. No matter what happens to me, please teach our child about Jesus Christ our Lord and Savior.

I'm going to Bible studies, so I can learn. Maybe I can lead someone to the Lord, too. Also, if for some reason the Lord takes me home, and He leads you to a new love, please don't be afraid to accept His direction. He will know what is best for you and our child. Just pray and ask His help. He will answer you. He will lead you, just lean on Him. Read your Bible and listen. I must go now. Duty calls. Each time you write, please send me pictures of you, so I can watch our baby grow inside you.

I'll end now so this letter will post today. Today is Friday, and no mail is picked up on the weekend.

Take care of our little one!
All my love,
Ken

Jerilyn placed her hand with care onto her stomach. "Dear Lord, is that my answer? Are you telling me to go to church and raise my child to know You? If You *are* guiding me, Lord, please just let me know Your wishes for me."

Jerilyn lay down on top of the bed, exhausted. She only intended to rest her eyes, but she fell asleep. She woke with a start and looked at her watch. It was almost time to head to the dining room. She changed her dress, washed her face, and then brushed her hair, twisting it back into the chignon. She checked herself in the mirror. Her dress looked fine. She had ironed it the night before. She knew she would need to make more dresses, but without a sewing machine it would take her a week to make at least one dress by hand. Her pregnancy did not show yet, but she knew it was only a matter of time. Her mother told her once she began to show when carrying Jerilyn, her stomach just popped out, seemingly overnight.

Jerilyn walked into the dining room right on time. Her eyes swept over the room as Christopher had taught her. She added two missing spoons on one table, a knife on another and one water glass. She noted a tablecloth had a stain on one corner and in an instant changed the cloth. Within twenty minutes, the room was perfect.

She seated the Bazells on the dot at five fifty-five. The other hotel guests began to file in and the waiters poured their water. Christopher and Lily arrived. Jerilyn started to seat them near the Bazells, but the Bazells motioned for them to dine at their table. Jerilyn whispered to Lily how pretty she looked in her blue dress and matching hair ribbons. Lily beamed and thanked her.

The evening went smoothly, and Christopher informed Jerilyn she had done a fine job. The Bazells nodded their approval.

Jerilyn finished at eight-thirty and slowly dragged her body up the stairs. It had been a long, but fulfilling day. As soon as she entered her room, she removed her dress and hung it in the armoire. She had been rotating her two good dresses and would need to wash and iron them to use for the following week. She also had the two uniforms and aprons for Mr. Blakely's diner she would need to wash and iron. She would be off on Saturday, so she planned to do the wash and ironing early that morning. She had not given Lily her answer about church. She thought about Ken's letter. *I don't suppose I should disappoint a little girl ... right, Lord?*

She decided she had done enough reading. Again, the letter to her parents would have to wait. The diary was safely in the secret drawer. She crawled into bed and turned out the light. This was the first night since Ken died that she could feel herself drifting into a peaceful sleep without distressing thoughts filling her mind.

Chapter Seven

New Friendships

"Thy word is a lamp unto my feet, and a light unto my path."
Psalm 119:105

Thursday Morning
December 18, 1941
Jerilyn awakened by four am, determined to write the letter to her parents and leave it at the front desk to be mailed.

Dear Mother and Father,
You will be able to tell by the postmark that I'm not in Nashville. I don't know where to begin, but my life is certainly different from when I left home early Monday morning. I am now beginning my fourth day in a small, quaint, lovely town called Franklin in Kentucky, and not Tennessee. However, I am six miles from the Tennessee border. Except for when I changed railroad lines in Louisville, I didn't get off the train at any of the stops until I reached Franklin, Kentucky. It was a

twenty-minute stop, so I thought I had enough time to use the facilities and have a snack. I finished a sandwich at the diner in the Franklin train station and discovered my purse was missing from within my suitcase. Someone must have removed it while I was on the train, as I never opened the case the whole journey. In the process of searching for my purse, the train left.

The waitress and manager at the diner were so kind to me. The manager, Mr. Blakely, told me the name of a hotel and wrote a note of introduction for me to the proprietors. Mr. Blakely said the proprietors of the hotel were friends of his, and would take care of me. Mr. Blakely even said he would give me a job at the diner, and I was to return in the morning if I was interested.

I walked the two blocks to Christmas Hotel and met Captain and Mrs. Bazell. They are very elderly, and they are very kind. They provided me with a room at the hotel and a job as the hostess during the supper shift. This hotel is so beautiful. They leave it decorated for Christmas all year around. The philosophy of the family that built this hotel in 1850 was that the miracles of Jesus Christ happen all year around, not just on the day we celebrate as His birth. Captain and Mrs. Bazell have carried on the tradition. I have heard people visit this beautiful hotel from many states.

On Tuesday morning I accepted the diner position. I work from 6 o'clock in the morning until 2 o'clock in the afternoon. Then I return to my room to rest before the supper shift at the hotel. I need to be on duty each evening from five-thirty until eight-thirty. Eleven hours a day does make for a long day, but it helps to have it broken up so I can rest in the afternoon. At both jobs I am off on Saturday and Sunday. The diner job gives me spending money, and the hostess job is in exchange for my room and board. I should be able to acquire a nice savings.

The hotel manager is Christopher Wright. He has been very helpful to me, teaching me my hostess duties. He has a darling five-year-old daughter whose name is Lily. She has breakfast with him each morning at the diner in the train station.

Well, I need to get to work at the diner. I will have the hotel post this letter today. Hopefully, you will have it by Monday or Tuesday. You can write to me at Christmas Hotel, Franklin, Kentucky.
Love,
Jerilyn

She stopped at the front desk, and the night clerk promised her letter would go out in the morning post. She arrived at the diner at the same time as Christopher and Lily.

Lily smiled, and said excitedly, "Good morning, Mrs. Seifert!"

"A very good morning to you, too, Miss Lily. By the way ... I've been thinking that Mrs. Seifert is way too formal for friends. Lily, would you please call me Miss Jerilyn? That is, if it's all right with your father."

Christopher nodded and smiled at Jerilyn. "I think that would be just fine." He took his coat and Lily's, hanging them on the wall hooks. By the time they reached the counter, Jerilyn had hung her coat in her locker room and was at the counter pouring Christopher's coffee. Nettie Sue already had a customer, but they greeted each other with a warm "hello".

"Are you having your usual hot chocolate this morning, Lily?"

"Yes, Miss Jerilyn. May I have a blueberry pancake and one scrambled egg, please?"

"If it's all right with your father." Jerilyn looked to Christopher who nodded in the affirmative.

"I'll have bacon with two scrambled eggs, and toast, please."

"I'll turn it in right away." She excused herself

to wait on two young men sitting on the adjacent stools.

To her dismay, one of them began flirting with her. She always felt uncomfortable receiving this sort of attention, even before she married Ken. Now, with both Christopher and Lily probably watching, she did her best to deal with it in a friendly, but professional manner, making sure they noticed her wedding band.

She could hear Lily's voice from the next stool as she poured the men more coffee. "Daddy, I asked you a question."

Jerilyn didn't intend to eavesdrop on the conversation, but their voices were loud enough to hear. Christopher said, "I'm sorry, sweetheart. What was the question?"

"Do you think it would be all right to ask Miss Jerilyn to take me Christmas shopping on Saturday? I've saved my allowance and I want to buy you a gift."

"I don't know, sweetheart. She may have plans. She has to work all week. She only has Saturday and Sunday off."

"I still want her to come to church and hear me sing on Sunday. May I ask her, and see what she says?"

"Well, I'll ask her about Saturday. *If* she will take you shopping, then *you* can ask her about church; but if she has plans on Saturday, *please* don't press her. All right?"

"All right, Daddy."

Jerilyn walked to the counter to replace the coffee pot, with the little girl's questions ringing in her head. Shopping would be fine, and after re-reading Ken's letter, maybe even church. She just couldn't disappoint Lily. She heard the two bells and picked up Christopher and Lily's breakfast. When she set down the plates, the two bells rang again. She delivered the breakfast for the two men. The flirtatious young man asked her what she was doing that evening.

She just smiled, and said, "I'm working my other job. Please excuse me."

"Wait! What are you doing on Saturday?" he pressed.

"I'll be back shortly," she said, and walked away.

She stopped in front of Christopher and Lily. Christopher evidently heard everything. He looked hesitant, but Lily tugged on his sleeve. "Ask her, please, Daddy?"

"Ahem," Christopher began, sounding nervous as he cleared his throat. "If you're not busy on Saturday, Lily was hoping ... if you have time, mind you ... that you might take her shopping for a Christmas present for me. Now, if you're busy, please just say so. She'll understand. Right, Lil–?"

He didn't have a chance to even finish his question for Lily, when Jerilyn interrupted. "I'll be happy to take Lily shopping. I'll need to wash and iron in the morning early, but I can be available around nine o'clock. Maybe we could go to lunch at Christmas Hotel, too. Would you like that, Lily?"

"Oh, Miss Jerilyn, I would love to!" She grinned so happily that Jerilyn's heart lurched.

"Well, it's a date then. Your daddy can drop you off at my room at nine o'clock on Saturday morning. We'll have some girl fun."

She grabbed the coffee pot and filled Christopher's cup and then the two men's. She answered the flirtatious young man by saying, "I already have a date on Saturday."

She looked back at Christopher who seemed pleased with the outcome of Lily's request. He and Lily finished their breakfast, he paid the check, and they said goodbye.

Chapter Eight

Unconditional Love

"If we confess our sins, he is faithful and just to forgive us our sins, and to cleanse us from all unrighteousness".
1 John 1:9

Thursday Evening
December 18, 1941
When Jerilyn finished her hostess duties, she hurried to her room, disappointed that Christopher and Lily had not taken dinner at the hotel that evening. He informed her earlier in the day that they would be staying home. He explained that Mrs. Evans, an older lady in town took care of Lily during the day while he was at work. The woman also cooked supper for them when they didn't eat at the hotel. Jerilyn still wondered about Christopher's wife.

She threw the lock on the door, unzipped her dress, slipped it off, and hung it in the armoire. She donned her gown and robe and hurried through her nightly routine: washed her face, brushed her hair, and then teeth. She opened the drapes so she could see the comforting gas lights and Christmas tree in the square. Retrieving the diary from the secret drawer, she sat curled up in a chair by the window, and began to read.

Monday, December 17, 1883 Carrie Emeline wrote: *I see things so differently. I have joy in my heart, and my parents are happy again. They just informed me they are purchasing Christmas Hotel. I couldn't be happier! I know a Christmas miracle has taken place in my heart.*

Tuesday, December 18, 1883 Carrie Emeline wrote: *My parents and Mr. and Mrs. Hoy met with the attorney today to transfer the deed. It seems the Simpson County Courthouse burned in May of 1882 and many documents were destroyed. The courthouse has since been restored, but Mr. Hoy has his personal copy of the deed. The attorney assures everyone there should be no problem transferring the title.*

Wednesday, December 19, 1883 Carrie Emeline wrote: *The attorney was correct. We are now the proud new owners of Christmas Hotel. This is a wonderful Christmas present for us as a family.*

Thursday, December 20, 1883 Carrie Emeline wrote: *Mr. and Mrs. Hoy hold a solid belief that the miracles of Jesus Christ should happen all year around, not just on the day we celebrate as his birth. My parents and I will carry on this tradition. This hotel will remain decorated for Christmas all year around. We hope when the guests visit, they will find their Christmas miracle ... as I have found mine. Thank You, Jesus.*

Jerilyn closed the diary. "Dear Lord, is this hotel my Christmas miracle, too? Did You lead me here to find this diary? I feel as if Carrie Emeline was just here last week, instead of fifty-eight years ago."

She rose, returned the diary to the desk, and opened the nightstand. She picked up the hotel's Bible and held it to her breast. "It's been a long time, Lord." She carried the Bible to the chair and sat. Scriptures from her youth came back to her mind in rapid order. John 14:1, Let not your heart be troubled: ye believe in God, believe also in me. John 14:18, I will not leave you comfortless: I will come to you. Psalm 30:8, I cried to thee, O Lord; and unto the Lord I made supplication. Psalm 35:27-28, Let them shout for joy, and be glad, that favour my righteous cause: yea, let them say continually, Let the Lord be magnified, which hath pleasure in the prosperity of his servant. And my tongue shall speak of thy righteousness and of thy praise all the day long. In 1 John 1:9: If we confess our sins, he is faithful and just to forgive us our sins, and to cleanse us from all unrighteousness.

Jerilyn bowed her head and prayed aloud. "*Lord, I'm sorry I have been away from You for so long, even though I know You have not been away from me. I love You, and I know You know what's best for me. Please help me move on beyond my grief. Let me find solace. Let me know the peace I once knew. Let me know Your wishes. Do You want me to give this baby up for adoption? Or do You want me to raise this baby? Please let me know Your will. I want to rededicate my life to You. I know now Ken's spirit is with You. If it is Your will, I will raise this child. I thank You for Your forgiveness and Your unconditional love for me.*"

A peace and overwhelming love filled her heart. She experienced a contentment that she had thought she would never feel again. *I feel as Carrie Emeline did, on December 17, 1883. I have joy in my heart again. A Christmas miracle has taken place in my heart, and hope resides once again.* She picked up her Bible and opened it to one of her favorite scriptures as a little girl: 2 Corinthians 12:9, 'And he said unto me, My grace is sufficient for thee: for my strength is made perfect in weakness. Most gladly therefore will I rather glory in my infirmities, that the power of Christ may rest upon me.'

She touched her stomach and smiled. "*Thank*

You, Jesus. I'm feeling Your healing hands. Thank You for helping me through my despair."

Chapter Nine

Gifts

"Draw nigh to God and he will draw nigh to you."
James 4:8

Friday Evening
December 19, 1941
The next day, Jerilyn finished both shifts and hurried up the stairs to her room. When she opened the door, she saw two pots of poinsettias: one on the nightstand and one on the desk. She walked to the one on the nightstand and found a card.

To Jerilyn, the best pupil I have trained in a long time. Thank you for your kindness toward my daughter Lily.
Fondly,
Christopher

Jerilyn smiled when she read the card and said aloud, "You are most welcome, Christopher."

The other pot sat on the desk. She picked up the card. The childish, but readable handwriting read:

Miss Jerilyn, thank you for being my friend.
Love,
Lily

Jerilyn held the card to her breast and began to cry. They signed the cards "fondly" and "love." *Dear Lord, my heart is falling for this family. Is this Your will? If not, please help me keep my emotions in check. It's too soon after Ken's death. I can't fall in love with this family. Help me know what to do.* She walked to the desk and retrieved the diary from the secret drawer.

Sunday, December 23, 1883 Carrie Emeline wrote: *I cannot believe I have missed two days writing in the diary. My life has been so eventful. My parents and I have been very busy learning about Christmas Hotel and how to run it the way the Hoy family did. The family has been kind enough to spend two weeks teaching us, before they bow out. Today we went to church and the sermon was on Luke chapter 2, which we have always called the Christmas Story. My father reads this to us every Christmas morning. Saint Nicholas is fun, but I must never forget the true meaning of Christmas. God joined his creation in the womb of a young virgin girl. He was the only baby ever born without sin. He was the sacrificial gift to His creation, so that I can live eternally wrapped in His loving arms.*

Jerilyn sat back and pondered Carrie Emeline's words. The next scripture that crossed her mind was John 3:16. *For God so loved the world, that he gave his only begotten son, that whosoever believeth in him should not perish, but have everlasting life.* How could she have wandered so far from the Savior?

She thought back to when she was born again at age eleven. She hadn't intended to drift from Him, but it happened. She wouldn't allow herself to look back, because she couldn't change her teen years. She would look forward to what God had planned for her future and her child's future. She held her stomach, smiled, and thanked God for His blessing and His precious gift. A part of Ken would live on.

Chapter Ten

Lily's Hope

"For in thee, O Lord, do I hope: thou wilt hear, O Lord my God."
Psalm 38:15

Saturday
December 20, 1941
Jerilyn awakened at four o'clock on Saturday morning, showered, and within thirty minutes was down in the hotel basement. After washing and drying her dresses, uniforms, aprons, and night gowns, she used the hotel's iron and ironing board, and finished by six-thirty. She had soaked her underclothes and stockings in the water closet's sink the night before, and now she hung them on her shower rod to dry. She brushed her hair and checked her face in the mirror, and noticed it looked plumper. She wondered if it was her new-found peace – or having to do with the baby.

She turned sideways to glance at her profile in the mirror. She smoothed her freshly pressed day dress over her body and felt a small bump. There was definitely a protrusion, and she knew her clothes would not fit much longer. She remembered her mom's words that her stomach seemed to pop out overnight when carrying her, so she decided to purchase the material and patterns for a couple of maternity outfits while shopping today with Lily.

Knowing she would need to be extra prudent with her money, she surmised she might be able to make one dress this week and another the following week. Sewing her own maternity clothes would save her a great deal of money instead of purchasing them off the hanger, but without a sewing machine it would take so much longer. Maybe she could find a used sewing machine that she could afford.

Eventually she would need to make clothes for the baby, too. Thankfully, her mother had taught her how to sew, knit, and crochet, and she would be putting those skills to use very soon. Even after her pregnancy began to show, she hoped the Bazells might continue to allow her to work in the dining room.; However, they may not want a woman in her condition greeting the customers. She also hoped Mr. Blakely would continue to allow her to work at the diner. She'd just have to cross that bridge when she came to it.

It was only seven o'clock, so she decided to read more entries from the diary before she went downstairs for a light breakfast. The diary was never far from her thoughts. Jerilyn now considered Carrie Emeline a sister from another century, and held a loving kinship with her.

December 24, 1883 Carrie Emeline wrote: *Today would have been my wedding day. It is sad, but I will lean on the Lord for comfort. The Lord's grace is sufficient for me.*

It is Christmas Eve and Christmas Hotel is fully booked. My parents and I have continued to stay in rooms 7 and 8. Sarah Hoy has been teaching me the duties of the hostess of the dining room.

"Sounds like me. How ironic," Jerilyn said aloud, with a smile.

Carrie Emeline continued. *I did not know there was so much to learn. My parents and I rarely went out to eat when we lived back in Rock Camp, Ohio. The nearest town with a fancy restaurant was Youngstown, and we only traveled there twice a year. My father will manage the hotel and work the front desk, while my mother will oversee the kitchen and housekeeping. This is a new experience for all of us, but we will learn. Tonight we will attend a Christmas concert at church.*

December 25, 1883 Carrie Emeline wrote: *Thank You, Lord Jesus, for coming to earth as a baby to save mankind. Thank You for saving my soul and rescuing me from my grief. I will always love Seth, but he is with You. I will see him again someday in eternity with You.*

Jerilyn glanced through the remainder of the year, noting that it just spoke about Carrie Emeline's daily duties, that is until New Year's Eve.

On December 31, 1883 Carrie Emeline wrote: *Well, today is the last day of 1883. This year was a long journey. One year ago I was the fiancée of Seth Johnson, the love of my life. When he died, I thought my life was over. I did not place my trust in You, Lord, to see me through the grief. My depression overwhelmed me and worried my parents. Thank You, Lord, for the parents You gave me. Thank You for answering their prayers for me. Thank You for Christmas Hotel. It is definitely blessed by You. I have found my miracle at Christmas Hotel. I know now that all things are possible with You, Lord. When our time is up on this earth, I pray You will position the right family to continue the traditions of Christmas Hotel. I pray that this hotel will provide blessings and inspiration for people for many years. Thank You for loving my family and allowing us to be the new proprietors of this amazing hotel. I pray for Your continued blessings on all the future guests who come here.*

Jerilyn closed the diary and placed it back in the secret compartment of the desk. *I wonder what happened the following year. I wish I had that diary, too.*

At eight-thirty she went down to breakfast, and to her surprise she saw Christopher and Lily seated at a table. Christopher rose and motioned to her to join them. He pulled out a chair for her and returned to his seat. The waiter arrived to pour her coffee and water.

"You're in time to order with us," said Christopher. "Lily and I just sat down."

They each gave their orders to the waiter. Jerilyn was the first to speak. "I want to thank you two for the lovely poinsettias I found in my room. It was very thoughtful," she said softly, looking from Christopher to Lily.

"My Daddy thought of it," piped up Lily. "We picked them out last night after dinner at the florist shop."

Jerilyn smiled at Christopher as Lily prattled on.

"My Daddy thought maybe you would come to dinner at our house tonight. Mrs. Evans is cooking roast beef with lots of vegetables and it's always good."

Jerilyn was unable to conceal her surprise at this announcement. Christopher seemed to notice.

"Honey, I thought we were going to wait until later today to ask Miss Jerilyn," he said, attempting to ease Jerilyn's discomfort.

Lily looked down into her lap. "I'm sorry, Daddy, I forgot." She looked up at her daddy sheepishly.

Jerilyn reached over and patted Lily's hand. "It's all right, Lily. I'd be very happy to have dinner with you this evening. Just give me the address, the time, and I'll be there."

Christopher handed her a slip of paper. He had already written 210 South College Street and six o'clock. Jerilyn read the slip of paper and stuck it in her pocket. "It's only two blocks from Christmas Hotel. You shouldn't have any trouble finding it."

After breakfast, Jerilyn and Lily said goodbye to Christopher and headed out to the shops. "What would you like to give your Daddy for Christmas?"

"He saw a sweater at *Draper and Darwin's Dry Goods*. I have enough money. We can buy some wrapping paper, too. Would you help me wrap it, Miss Jerilyn?"

"I'd be happy to, honey."

Snow began to fall, and Jerilyn stopped to adjust Lily's scarf to protect her neck and face. She pulled Lily's hat down over her ears, and then they hurried to the dry goods store, stamping the snow from their boots before entering. The sweaters were in the front of the store and Lily walked directly to the display with the pattern she wanted to purchase for her father.

She looked through the stack of sweaters, and then looked up at Jerilyn. "I didn't think about size," she said with a trembling lip. A tear escaped from her right eye and trailed down her cheek. "What should I do?"

Jerilyn bent down and hugged the distraught little girl. "Don't worry, sweetheart. I think I can figure this out for you," she said, as she gently wiped the tear from Lily's cheek with her finger. She thought about Ken and Christopher's build. Ken had a thirty-four inch waist, and a forty-four inch chest. He was six feet two inches tall. She estimated Christopher about the same size. Jerilyn stood, found a large sweater, and handed it to Lily. "This will fit your daddy."

Lily smiled. "Thank you, Miss Jerilyn!"

Next they picked out the wrapping paper and ribbon, and carried everything to the counter for Lily to purchase. As the man behind the counter rang up the order, Jerilyn observed that the cash register was manufactured by NCR. Something built in Dayton was right here in front of her. It didn't make her homesick, and when she realized that fact, it didn't sadden her either. She had found a new contentment in her alternate home in Franklin.

Jerilyn spent the next hour picking out items she needed: fabrics, thread, a maternity dress pattern, a purse, and a wallet. She hoped to borrow a needle, thimble, pins, and sewing scissors from Mrs. Bazell. After choosing enough material for two day dresses, she decided to wait until after receiving next week's pay to purchase the material for two evening dresses. Anyway, the evening dresses wouldn't be necessary if the Bazells didn't want her to hostess after her pregnancy began to show. She also wanted to send a present to her parents, although she knew even if it posted on Monday, it would not arrive before Christmas. She bought a small drawing of the square and Christmas Hotel that she would give to them next time they met. She purchased plenty of yarn to crochet scarves for her Franklin, Kentucky friends for Christmas. Hopefully, Mrs. Bazell would have a crochet hook she could borrow.

Before they left the store, Jerilyn noticed a used, but in very good condition, Singer sewing machine, black with gold decorations, and in a lovely wooden case. Although used, the cost was still eight dollars, and she just couldn't afford to spend that much of her carefully budgeted money.

Lily watched as Jerilyn touched the machine. "Is that what you want for Christmas, Miss Jerilyn?"

"Oh, honey, that's much too expensive. I would never expect anyone to spend that amount of money. Besides, I'm a good seamstress. I can make my own clothes by hand. It will just take longer."

By the time they finished their shopping, it was eleven-thirty. The snow still came down in a white cloud, and they bundled up and headed back toward Christmas Hotel. On the lobby mat they stamped the snow off their feet, and then hurried up the stairs to Jerilyn's room. They laid all the packages on the bed, and removed their outerwear.

Jerilyn clapped her hands with excitement. "Let's go have some lunch. We can come back later and wrap your daddy's sweater."

When they entered the dining room, they saw the Bazells seated at their personal table, and they waved for Jerilyn and Lily to come over.

"Please join us," said Mrs. Bazell. "We would love the company."

"Thank you, Mrs. Bazell. We'd love to join you... right, Lily?"

Lily answered with her usual enthusiasm. "Yes, I love Mr. and Mrs. Bazell!"

"Mrs. Bazell patted the chair beside her and motioned for Lily to sit beside her. "And we love you too, Miss Lily."

Jerilyn and Lily sat, and the waiter took their orders. They each asked for grilled cheese sandwiches and tomato soup. Lily politely folded her hands in her lap, and Jerilyn thought again how well-behaved Lily was. Her dad had taught her well.

"What have you ladies been doing this morning?" Captain Bazell asked.

Lily bubbled over with excitement when she told the Bazells about shopping with Jerilyn for her gift for her daddy.

"Lily, what would *you* like for Christmas?" asked Mrs. Bazell.

Lily paused for a moment, mulling over the question. Then very softly she answered, "I want a mommy."

The three at the table grew quiet.

Lily continued, "I didn't get to know my mommy. When I visit my best friend Ruth at her home, her mommy is so nice. Her mommy hugs her a lot and kisses her. She tells her how much she loves her. She smells really nice. They do things together like shopping and baking. Ruth said they were going to bake Christmas cookies today. Mrs. Evans is nice and she can cook and bake, but she's old, and she already has a family. She's someone else's mommy, and a grandma too. I know she loves my daddy and me, but it's not the same. I want my own mommy."

When she finished speaking, Jerilyn had to turn her head so no one would notice as she wiped a tear from her eye. When she looked back, she saw that Mrs. Bazell was watching her. Jerilyn returned Mrs.

Bazell's gaze and then bowed her head.

Their food had arrived and Captain Bazell asked the blessing, while Jerilyn thought about Lily's longing. She prayed silently for Lily. *Lord, I pray You will bless Lily with the desires of her little heart, and find her the right mommy.*

Chapter Eleven

Loves Lost

"The righteous cry, and the Lord heareth, and delivereth them out of all their troubles."
Psalm 34:17

Saturday Eve
December 20, 1941
Jerilyn arrived at the Wright home promptly at six o'clock. A mixture of huge old black and white oak trees lined the street. Christopher and Lily lived in a lovely two-story pale yellow frame home with deep green shutters and a dark brown roof. Two shade trees covered the front yard, and a brick walkway led from the sidewalk to the front steps. Jerilyn was impressed with the beautiful old, but well-maintained home. Four holly-wrapped columns surrounded the front door, that supported the walk-out balcony immediately above, with an additional four columns around the balcony. Strings of twinkling lights encompassed the two windows on each side of the front door and the windows beside the balcony. Block window lights vertically lined both sides of the front door, with a stained-glass transom above the door. The two

coach lanterns on each side of the block window lights were both lit. Jerilyn chuckled at the double meaning when she saw the oak sign below one lantern: The Wright Family. In the window to the left of the front door, a Christmas tree twinkled brightly.

She climbed the six steps leading up to the entrance and lightly rapped using the brass knocker. A small dog barked inside the home.

Christopher greeted her with a huge smile. "Welcome to our home, Jerilyn."

Lily rushed to the door before Jerilyn could speak. She hugged Jerilyn around her knees, saying excitedly, "Thank you for coming!" She grasped Jerilyn's hand pulling her into the house.

Christopher grinned, and shrugged his shoulders.

"I want you to meet my dog Daisy," said Lily. "She's a Cocker Spaniel. Sit, Daisy!"

The dog obediently sat in front of Lily and Jerilyn, and wagged its stubby tail.

"She'll shake your hand if you put your hand out and say, 'Daisy shake.'" Lily looked up at Jerilyn. "If you'd rather not, that's okay, too," she added quickly.

"I'd love to shake Daisy's paw," said Jerilyn. She put out her hand. "Daisy, shake!"

The dog stuck out her paw and Jerilyn shook it.

Jerilyn and Christopher laughed when Lily said, "Good dog, Daisy!" and she gave Daisy a treat.

"All right, honey," said Christopher. "Now that Jerilyn has officially met Daisy, let's put Daisy in the basement while we eat."

Lily dutifully called Daisy in through the dining room and opened the door into what Jerilyn assumed was the kitchen that probably led to the basement. Her home in Dayton had a similar floor plan.

Mrs. Evans set the steaming platter with the roast on the table in the dining room adjoining the living room. She wiped her hands on her apron, and Christopher introduced her to Jerilyn. "Jerilyn Seifert, I would like you to meet the wonderful lady who takes care of us, Mrs. Evans. Mrs. Evans, I would like you to meet our new friend, Jerilyn Seifert."

The ladies shook hands pleasantly.

Mrs. Evans addressed Christopher. "The dinner is ready and on the table. I've already eaten, so if you'll excuse me I will retire upstairs to the guest room. I have some Christmas cards to write, and I would like to listen to the Grand Ole Opry on the radio while you and Lily entertain Jerilyn. Please call me if you need anything."

"I will," said Christopher. "Thank you so much for cooking the meal."

After Mrs. Evans closed her door to the guest room, Christopher turned to Jerilyn. “Mrs. Evans is truly a blessing for us. Without her help, I don’t know what we’d do. She rarely spends the night, but said she would tonight and stay with Lily, so that I’d be able to walk you back to Christmas Hotel. Anyway, let’s not allow this wonderful dinner to get cold.”

They walked into the dining room and Christopher seated Jerilyn and then Lily. Mrs. Evans had placed a white cloth on the table with a red and green cloth runner, and a centerpiece of two red candles in silver holders on either side of a poinsettia. A platter held a sliced steaming roast and side bowls with carrots, onions, turnips, squash, and roasted potatoes, along with what Christopher said was Mrs. Evans’ famous Southern cornbread. At each dinner plate, Mrs. Evans had set a red and green fruit salad, and a large glass of sweet tea.

Christopher sat down at the head of the table, and taking the hands of Jerilyn and Lily, bowed his head, and asked the blessing.

When he finished, Lily began to tell him about their day. She omitted that she had purchased the sweater, but did blurt out about the sewing machine. “When we were leaving the store, Miss Jerilyn saw a sewing machine, but she said she really didn't need one. She said she sewed well enough by hand, just that it took longer."

After dinner, they all three cleared the table, and carried the dirty dishes into the kitchen. They wrapped the platter and bowls of the leftover food in cellophane, and set them in the electric Frigidaire. The three of them washed, dried, and put away the dishes. Jerilyn thought about this familial scene. When she was growing up, her parents did the same thing with her after their evening meal. Lily reminded her so much of herself at that age. When she and Ken were first married, the two of them did the same, until he left for the Navy. *I miss this*, she thought. *I miss being in a family. I suppose I didn't comprehend how lonely I really am.*

After they cleaned the kitchen, they made hot chocolate with marshmallows on top, let Daisy out of the basement, and retired to the living room. Jerilyn glanced around the spacious and homey living room. Ornate, natural light oak woodwork bordered the high ceilings, and a beautifully carved staircase led up to the second floor. A multitude of pictures were scattered around the lovely room, some on the cherry tables and some on the walls, and were mostly of Lily at every age. In one baby picture of Lily, she was held by Christopher with an older couple standing beside them. In another picture, Christopher held Lily's hand, obviously learning to walk. On the grand piano set a picture of Christopher in an army uniform with his arm around a beautiful woman with long black wavy hair; possibly a wedding picture, she wondered?

When they finished their hot chocolate, Christopher sat on the bench at the highly polished piano, and Lily sat beside him. He motioned for Jerilyn to join them. She stood beside the piano while he opened his hymn book and he, along with Lily accompanying him, played "O Come, All Ye Faithful", and the three of them sang. Jerilyn chose next with "It Came upon the Midnight Clear", and Lily chose "O Little Town of Bethlehem". Christopher ended with "Silent Night".

Jerilyn applauded Christopher and Lily. "How long has Lily played piano?"

Christopher thought for a moment. "She was just past two when she asked me to teach her, so three years."

"Lily, you play beautifully."

Lily beamed from the compliment. "Thank you, Miss Jerilyn."

Christopher checked his watch, looked to Jerilyn and then to Lily, and addressed Lily. "Lily honey, it's time for bed."

A sad look crossed Lily's face.

Christopher continued, "Maybe we can get Miss

Jerilyn to help you into your gown tonight and watch you brush your teeth, and I'll join you two soon."

Lily's face brightened, and she jumped down from the piano bench, grabbed Jerilyn's hand, and pulled her to the stairway.

Ten minutes later Jerilyn and Lily sat on the edge of the bed. Jerilyn brushed Lily's hair, and Lily hugged her. "I'm glad you're here, Miss Jerilyn. My daddy is tired so much, but he wasn't tonight. He was happy. I think he likes you. I like you, too."

Jerilyn smiled and returned the hug. "I like you too, sweetheart," she answered softly. "What's next in your bedtime ritual?"

"I need to say my prayers, and Daddy always listens. Then he tucks me in and reads to me until I fall asleep."

Christopher walked into the room, and hugged Lily. Jerilyn got the impression he might have been waiting outside the door, and was pretending he had just arrived, so as not to embarrass her.

"Well, Lily, are you ready to say your prayers?"

"Yes, Daddy. Will you listen to my prayers, too, Miss Jerilyn?"

Jerilyn looked to Christopher for confirmation. He nodded, so all three knelt on the floor beside the bed with Lily in the middle. I can't have Lily get too attached to me, thought Jerilyn. I may still move on to Nashville or return home to Dayton, and I don't want to break her heart."

"Dear Heavenly Father, thank You for bringing Miss Jerilyn to Franklin. Daddy and I like her and I think she likes us. I really liked Christmas shopping with her today. She's fun ... just like Ruth's mommy. I like it when she hugs me, and she smells really nice. God, please bless Miss Jerilyn, my daddy, and Mrs. Evans, and Daisy. Oh, and Miss Jerilyn said the sewing machine was expensive, but Daddy says all things are possible with You. Please give her that sewing machine for Christmas; and God ... if it's not too much trouble, please give me a mommy for Christmas. In the name of your Son Jesus I pray ... Amen."

Christopher hugged Lily when she finished, and Jerilyn felt it necessary to look away. She sniffed and wiped a tear. *Children's prayers could be so open and honest, with no pretense.* Christopher picked up Lily and laid her in the bed, placing her head on the propped pillows. He walked around on the other side and Jerilyn helped tuck her in.

Christopher pulled up the chair and Jerilyn sat on the bed beside Lily. "All right, Lily," he said, "what story do you want to hear tonight?

"Would you read me *Curious George*, please?"

"My dear Lily, I think I have read you that story twenty times since we bought it at the bookstore this year. I'd think you would have it memorized."

"All right, Daddy. Maybe Miss Jerilyn could read the story tonight. Then it will sound different!"

Jerilyn and Christopher laughed as he pulled the book from the bookshelf and handed it to Jerilyn. Within five minutes Lily was fast asleep. Christopher kissed her on the forehead, turned out the light, and they tiptoed from the room, closing the door.

When they reached the bottom of the steps, Christopher asked Jerilyn to stay a while longer, and promised he would then walk her back to the hotel. She agreed. Christopher selected a Christmas album and put it on the record player, while Jerilyn made more hot chocolate. Returning to the living room, they took seats in chairs facing each other. Daisy lay on the floor at Christopher's feet, chewing on her rubber bone, and Jerilyn removed her shoes, curling her legs under her.

"I never appreciated restaurant workers before, as I should have," she said. "The long hours at the diner and the hotel dining room do make my feet ache." She reached down and rubbed her left foot. "Working in the office at National Cash Register in Dayton, I sat most of the day. I'm not complaining. I love the work here, and I love the people I've met."

"Do you think you'll stay in Franklin or continue

on to Nashville?"

"I like this little town. I've only been here a short time, but I already feel at home. At the present time, I've no intentions of continuing on to Nashville. I needed the change. My spirits have definitely been lifted in this past week. However, at some point, I'd like to visit Ken's family in Nashville, whom I've never had the opportunity to meet. "She looked at him intently, and asked pointedly, "Christopher, do you believe in miracles?"

He gazed back at her just as intense. "As Lily prayed in her prayer tonight ... I believe all things are possible with God. There was a time though I nearly lost my faith." He lowered his head.

"Would you tell me about Lily's mother?" she asked gently.

He sighed. "Yes, I'd like to talk about her with you." He paused, looked to the ceiling as if for inspiration, and returned his gaze toward Jerilyn. "Her name was Eleanor Simmons, but she was always called Ellie. Right after high school in 1931, I left Franklin and enlisted for four years in the army, in its air corps division. I was stationed in the Philippines at Clark Field. My unit didn't have a chaplain, and therefore, since I was the only man with Bible training, I became the chaplain for my unit. At the time, I felt the call to preach, so I knew it was the Lord's will. It was a different time then, because the world was at peace."

He paused a moment, as though realizing his statement might cause Jerilyn pain, but she nodded for him to continue.

"There were some missionaries living nearby and that's how I met Ellie. Ellie and her parents were missionaries. They were holding a revival, and some of the men in my unit and I showed up. Ellie's father preached the first night of the revival. I spoke with her parents afterwards, and invited them to our base the following day for a tour. I must admit my motives were somewhat selfish. I really wanted to get to know Ellie.

"After that night, we saw each other as much as possible. Two months later we were married at the mission by her father, Pastor Simmons." He pointed to the picture of him with the woman with long black hair. "That's Ellie with me, and that was our wedding day."

Jerilyn looked at the picture which now confirmed her original suspicion.

"I was granted permission to live off base at the mission camp, but I was required to return to the base each day. When my four year tour was up, we considered staying on at the mission, or upping for another tour of duty, but Ellie was then pregnant with Lily. We prayed and felt led to move home to

Franklin." He looked to Jerilyn to see if she was really interested in his story and received confirmation with her gaze and tender smile.

"Dad and Mom Simmons promised to come to Franklin the month before Lily was born. They wanted to be present for the birth of their first grandchild, and I wanted our child to know his or her grandparents. Both of my parents were dead, killed in an automobile accident during my senior year in high school. That's a story I'll tell you about at another time."

"I would like to hear that story, too," Jerilyn said with encouragement and assuring him that she wanted to know more about his life.

"Two weeks before Ellie's due date, she went into labor. Something was wrong. She became nauseous, began vomiting, and had a severe headache. Dad and Mom Simmons stayed with Ellie while I ran to get Dr. Beasley. When Dr. Beasley arrived, he quickly assessed the situation. We carried Ellie upstairs. She was able to deliver Lily, and then I watched her slip into a coma, never to awaken. Ellie was gone within a few minutes. Dr. Beasley said it was a condition called eclampsia. If she hadn't been in the last stage of delivery, and they had been in a hospital, he would have performed a cesarean section, and Ellie may have lived.

"One month before she died, we discussed names for the baby. If the baby was a boy, he'd be named after me. If the baby was a girl, she'd be named for Ellie's favorite flower, the Easter Lily, because Ellie was due around Easter. Lily was born on Easter Sunday, April 12, 1936." He stopped speaking for a moment, and all was quiet except for the record playing in the background.

As soon as Jerilyn felt she could control her speech, she managed to say, "Christopher ... I'm so sorry. What you must have gone through."

"All I can say was I was blessed to have the support and prayers of Ellie's parents and Mrs. Evans. Without them, I don't know what I would have done. The first week, I was terribly depressed and mad at God. I kept asking why, God? I'm ashamed to say I even had trouble looking at Lily. I blamed her for Ellie's death ... and I blamed God. Mom Simmons and Mrs. Evans took charge of Lily."

"I understand completely. I had the same feelings after Ken's death," she said as she wiped a tear that escaped down her cheek. "Please continue Christopher," she added softly.

"About a week later, Dad Simmons approached me. In a loving, but stern way, he told me I had to snap out of the depression I had spiraled into. He didn't mince words, because he knew I was in trouble – therefore, so was his granddaughter. I was on the verge of losing my sanity, and Dad Simmons knew it. We talked all one day and well into the night. He helped bring me back from the brink of disaster. He reminded me as long as there is sin in the world there will be situations none of us can control. We don't know why bad things will happen to good people. He said that was something he intended to ask the Lord when he was called home. He also added that if every situation went exactly as we would like it to, we wouldn't need a Lord and Savior.

"He said there would be mountain tops and valleys in the life of a Christian. The Lord had something for us to learn while in the valley, and we'd never reach the mountaintop again until we did. He said if I allowed the Lord to help me, He would see me through this. Ellie was with the Lord. Her battles were over. Mine would remain for the rest of my life, as life wasn't always fair. Dad Simmons reminded me the Lord would never leave me or forsake me. He would always be with me. I just needed to lean on Him."

Jerilyn withdrew her handkerchief from her pocket and dabbed at her eyes.

"I must say losing my parents had been painful, but it didn't prepare me for losing Ellie. However, Dad Simmons got through to me. I finally realized I had an obligation to raise Lily to know the Lord. She was my responsibility, not the responsibility of Mom Simmons or Mrs. Evans. Yes, Ellie wouldn't be with me to share this precious gift, therefore Lily was now *my* duty, and Lily needed me. Dad Simmons told me I had to be a good father for the sake of Lily. Dad Simmons's words finally sunk in, and I was able to pray with him. Then together we knelt and recited the Twenty-third Psalm. It took on new meaning for me. I rose from that prayer and recitation, and walked upstairs to the nursery where Lily slept in her cradle. Mom Simmons was asleep in a roll-away bed we'd set up, so she could be near Lily. A nightlight lit the room.

"I walked to the cradle and looked down at my daughter. Picking her up, I sat down in the rocker. There was a table beside the rocker with a lamp that I turned on the lowest notch so as not to disturb Mom Simmons. I held my daughter as she slept, and examined her face for the first time. She had Ellie's nose and chin. Her face had my high cheek bones and her hair was curly and brown like mine when I was a child. My hair was once as curly as Lily's, but it has relaxed into waves over the years. I counted all her fingers and toes. She had Ellie's slender fingers. I bent my head and prayed for my daughter as the tears fell on her blanket.

"Mom Simmons heard me. She rose and knelt

on the floor in front of me. She held my hand, and one of Lily's, and prayed for the both of us. My life changed that night. I asked God to forgive me for my anger, and He did. His peace and love enveloped me. The next day I heard about the manager's position at Christmas Hotel, and I applied. Mr. and Mrs. Bazell hired me, and my life has been blessed.

"I thank the Lord every day for Lily, the Bazells, my in-laws, and for Mrs. Evans. His grace sustains me. I'm now twenty-eight years old, and He never ceases to amaze me. In answer to your question, do I believe in miracles? I will answer with a resounding *yes*! *All* things are possible with God. However, I'm sorry I made you cry. That was certainly not my intention."

"Christopher, I am honored that you told me the story. I now feel as if I know Ellie. Thank you for sharing with me."

Christopher looked intently at her and asked, "Now I've bared my soul to you, will you honor me with hearing your story?"

Jerilyn stared into Christopher's eyes. She felt a connection with him and wanted to tell him of her life. She took a deep breath and began.

"You already know my husband Ken was killed at Pearl Harbor. Just for a little background information, Ken, my best friend Emma, and her future husband Jack, and I, all attended Theodore Roosevelt High School in Dayton, Ohio. We were inseparable the entire four years. My parents raised me in church, but I didn't attend after marriage because Ken didn't go, although Emma and Jack did. Life seemed to be just fine for Ken and me without God and church.

"On Sunday afternoon, December seventh, my life abruptly changed, as did the lives of all of us in America. I sat listening to classical music on the radio while reading a book of baby names given to me by Emma. My mother told me she'd heard that classical music soothed the soul of the baby in the womb." She paused a moment and cupped her stomach. "You see, I'm going to have Ken's baby." She tried to make it sound very matter-of-fact.

Christopher didn't act as if this was a problem or seem surprised. Instead, he nodded with understanding, so she continued. "I was drawing two columns on the sheet of paper: one for boys' names and one for girls' names. My parents invited me to church that morning, and as usual, I declined.

"CBS radio correspondent Charles Daly suddenly interrupted the program. I listened to his announcement that the Japanese had attacked Pearl Harbor, and time seemed to stop. All I could think was that Ken's ship was stationed there. I heard nothing beyond the announcement. I looked at the clock and it was two thirty-one in the afternoon. I remember placing my hand on my stomach. I was paralyzed with fear. The sound of the radio now droned from far away, although it was in the same room as I.

"I thought I must be dreaming and would awaken and all would be all right with the world. Then the ringing of the telephone interrupted my thoughts. Deep down, I knew Ken had been killed. Nothing was going to convince me otherwise. I stood on wobbly legs, and holding one piece of furniture to the next, I stumbled into the entry hall. I held onto the wall as I sat down at the telephone stand.

"I picked up the receiver. 'Hello.' I didn't recognize my own voice. I guess I spoke so softly I couldn't be heard. It was Emma on the phone. 'Jerilyn, can you hear me? Do you have the radio on?' I struggled to find words. My head was spinning. I was dazed, but I managed to respond to her. 'Yes. Pearl Harbor has been bombed. Ken's there.' I know that I spoke so slow and calm that I worried her. She said, 'I heard the announcement too, and I'm catching the next trolley to come and stay with you.'

"I remained at the telephone stand after Emma

and I said goodbye. Within moments my front door burst open, and in walked my parents who lived three houses away from our home. They took one look at me and knew I'd heard the news. They knelt on the floor and held me. That's all I needed to snap out of my shock. The tears flowed and I heard a sound that seemed to come from a wounded animal. Then I realized it was me. They held me as I cried until my throat was raw and the tears were gone. Emma arrived, and they walked me upstairs to my room."

She looked at Christopher, took a breath and sighed. It was hard to relive the moment, but when he nodded Jerilyn knew he understood.

"Because I was pregnant, they didn't want to call the doctor to give me a sedative. I awakened several times in the night and my parents and Emma were by my side. They had dragged extra chairs into my room and lined them up beside my bed. I don't think any of them slept that night. I saw them several times in the night huddled together in prayer, and then I'd fall back into a restless sleep. I know they worried about me and the baby.

"The official telegram arrived, and the memorial service was held on Friday, December twelfth which was also Ken's and my second wedding anniversary. It was that evening that I decided to go to Nashville. Ken had family in Nashville and I felt that looking them up would allow me to feel closer to Ken. I informed my parents the next day of my decision. I bought my tickets and boarded the early morning one o'clock train Monday, December fifteenth. Although they pleaded with me not to leave, I was adamant. My parents and Emma saw me off.

Jerilyn paused for a moment and Christopher waited silently for her to continue when she was ready.

Jerilyn inhaled deeply and then released her breath. "To back up and give you some history before that 'day of infamy,' I came to know Jesus as my Savior at the age of eleven, but in high school I gradually drifted away from the Lord. I was born and raised in Dayton, Ohio, and Ken moved to Dayton from Nashville, Tennessee, his freshman year. His father moved the family there for an executive position at National Cash Register, or more commonly known as NCR. Ken and I were smitten with each other from the day we first met. Our lockers were side-by-side for homeroom. He tried out for football and I for cheerleading. By our senior year, he was the captain of the football team and I was the head cheerleader.

"We never quarreled or dated anyone else. We knew it was as if we were meant for each other. However, my parents worried about the union with

Ken, because he wasn't a Christian. They thought he'd continue to steer me away from God. I didn't care, as I decided I didn't need the Lord's help to make my decisions. By the time I was out of high school I felt as if I was an adult, and free to marry Ken when he proposed marriage. We were married on December 12, 1939.

"However, jobs were scarce, and Ken had no desire to work at NCR. He heard that if he enlisted for four years, we'd have the United States Navy benefits. He joined and was assigned to work in the medical unit on his ship. Ken always wanted to be a doctor and he didn't want to burden his parents to pay for his college. The Navy promised him an internship on his ship, and when his four years were finished, they'd pay to complete his education. He thought I might even be able to join him when he was stationed on land. We agreed this was a good decision for our future. Of course we didn't expect December seventh to happen either.

"After Ken's memorial service last week, as I said before, my parents begged me not to leave home. They didn't think it wise to make such a decision so soon after Ken's death. They wanted to be there for me, all through the pregnancy. I wanted a change. I *needed* a change. I couldn't bear being in the house I shared with Ken, and I knew I could no longer live with my parents. Ken's parents, like your parents, had met an untimely death. They both contracted influenza and died shortly after Ken and I married. He had family in Nashville, and he told me many stories of his upbringing. He always promised to take me there to meet his family, but we never had the chance."

She paused a moment before speaking again.

"You know, a week ago, I was like you after Ellie died. I was a broken woman, but God pulled me out of my despair. I'm not saying my heart is healed, but it's better. God wanted me in Franklin, Kentucky at Christmas Hotel. I found my miracle here at Christmas Hotel. I believe I was brought here for 'such a time as this,' as Esther in the Bible said. Since arriving here, I've rededicated my life and heart to God, and the extreme depression has lifted. Five days ago I had even thought about giving my baby up for adoption."

She cupped her stomach and looked down. A moment later she looked back at Christopher, and smiled through watery eyes. "I know now that I cannot possibly give up this precious gift from the Lord. Whatever shall befall me, I will lean on Him."

"I understand completely," Christopher replied, nodding wisely. "God has a way of changing the hearts of his children. Remember what I told you about learning in the valleys before you can get back on the mountaintop? My father-in-law was right about that." Then he asked her directly, "Do you know if Ken was saved before he died?"

She smiled. "Yes, he was. He wrote me about it in his last letter, which I received after his death. I can rest assured he's with God."

"That's something for which we both can be assured. At least we know we'll see them again. We can thank God for His blessed assurance."

"You know, Christopher, I could talk to you all night, but I'd like to be fresh in the morning. I'm looking forward to Lily singing in the church program."

Christopher looked at his watch and nodded in agreement. "You're right. I think I could talk all night, too. The time has passed much too quickly."

They rose, and Jerilyn put her shoes back on. He helped her with her coat.

When they arrived back at the hotel, she said, "Thank you for inviting me to dinner, Christopher. I enjoyed our conversation. You don't know how much talking about Ken has helped me, as well as hearing about you and Ellie. Ken was my life for most of my teen years, and although for two years he has been away, except for a couple of leaves of absence, and I have been alone, I did not feel lonely. We definitely were not a normal married couple, because he joined the Navy soon after our marriage. We really didn't have time to settle in a routine as a normal married couple would, but I always knew that he was as close as a letter.

"Carrying our child also, has made me feel close to him. I really have had no one to talk with about Ken. My friends and family knew and loved him, so it was hard to discuss my feelings without also causing them grief. They naturally wanted to comfort me, but I needed someone to talk to. Thank you for the opportunity. Just listening has helped me more that you know."

"Jerilyn, I feel the same way. It was the same for me. Although I finally came to my senses after Ellie's death, I really had no one to pour out my heart and feelings. Thank you for listening. I feel as though this moment was meant for both of us."

He cleared his throat and took her hand. "Maybe now is not the right time, but when you're ready, I'd like to court you. Please just let me know when the time is right."

She looked into his kind and compassionate eyes. "I will. I'll see you and Lily in the morning for breakfast before church."

She released his hand, turned and walked up the staircase of Christmas Hotel. When she reached the top of the staircase, she sensed she was being watched from below. She looked down into the lobby and saw the Bazells with their backs to her, quietly hobbling into their office.

Chapter Twelve

Lily's Church Concert

"And let the peace of God rule in your hearts to the which also ye are called in one body; and be ye thankful."
Colossians 3:15

Sunday morning
December 21, 1941
Jerilyn awakened in a happier mood; a burden on her heart had been lifted following the long conversation with Christopher. She stretched her long arms, grabbed her robe, and stepped into her slippers. Rushing to the window, she threw open the drapes to see the sun just peeking over the trees in the square, and a light snow falling, adding to the three inches already on the ground. Opening the french doors, she stepped out onto the balcony and inhaled a deep breath of the cold fresh air. A few people entered the nearby churches on the square, and she assumed they were probably people warming the buildings for the early Sunday morning services. The pristine snow on the walks

and streets had not yet been tainted by the automobiles and footprints.

"Thank You, Lord, for bringing me here," she prayed audibly.

She stepped back into the room and closed the doors. From her armoire she selected her navy blue suit with a white ruffle blouse to wear to church, and hung it on the door to the water closet. She showered, brushed her teeth and hair, and applied a light pink lipstick. She slipped into her underclothes, but when she began to zip her skirt, she realized she would not be able to zip it all the way. She pulled her blouse over the top of the skirt to hide the top of the zipper. Closing her eyes, she caressed the swell that was the miracle of her child. *Ken will live on. He will not be forgotten.*

When she arrived in the dining room, she found the Bazells, Christopher, and Lily already waiting for her at the Bazells' table. Christopher stood and held her chair. "Thank you, Christopher."

Lily jumped up and hugged her. "Good morning, Miss Jerilyn. I'm so happy you're going to church with us. I hope you like the children's' program. We have all rehearsed a *very* long time."

"I'm sure I'll love it." Lily sat back down, and Christopher whispered to Jerilyn that the rehearsals had taken all of two weeks; a *very* long time to a five-year old.

Lily wore a red dress with white lace trim around the cuffs and the hem. A red bow adorned her curly hair and a black belt and black leather boots finished her outfit. Perfectly adorable, thought Jerilyn.

Immediately, the waiter arrived to hand them menus. "We have omelets any way you want them, which is the hotel's weekend special. I'll give you time to decide your order and return shortly." At that, the busy waiter quickly moved to another table.

Christopher turned to Jerilyn. "On the weekend, you'll not only see the hotel guests, but many of the townspeople show up for breakfast, especially on Sunday morning before church. As you can see, the dining room is already full. By the way, the omelets really are amazing."

"Well, in that case, I'll have to try one." When the waiter returned she ordered the omelet with ham, cheese, tomatoes, and red peppers. I hope the red peppers aren't too much for the baby, she thought to herself.

Following breakfast, Christopher slowly walked arm-in-arm with Captain and Mrs. Bazell on either side of him, while Jerilyn walked ahead with Lily. Christopher had offered to drive the Bazells, but they wanted to walk. "We like to greet the people on the square," Mrs. Bazell said with that amazing twinkle in her eye. Lily was excited, as always, with the snow, and doing her typical Lily bounce, as Christopher called it

Looking up at Jerilyn she asked, "Miss Jerilyn, will you have the noon meal at Christmas Hotel after church with us? After we eat, we're going to make igloos in the square! Doesn't that sound like fun?"

Jerilyn looked back at Christopher, who had obviously heard the question. He laughed. "Well, doesn't that sound like fun, Jerilyn? We can build a snowman, and if you're lucky, you'll probably get a snowball or two thrown at you. You can't pass up an offer like that." He grinned as he winked at Jerilyn.

Jerilyn laughed too. "I suppose I can't. Lily, I'd be honored to have the noon meal with you and play in the snow afterwards."

They entered the church and Christopher hung all their coats, hats, and scarves in the foyer closet. After introducing Jerilyn to Pastor Palmer and his wife Mary, he seated Jerilyn and the Bazells near the front row, and he explained he was taking Lily around behind the stage to get ready for her singing. No electric lights were used today, just candles lit the sanctuary.

Christopher returned to the sanctuary and took

his seat beside Jerilyn. The curtain opened to the live nativity scene in front of them, and alongside that, the four risers of children age four to twelve. Lily had been placed in the front row with all the other small children. When Lily saw them she waved excitedly, and they returned the wave.

Many older children were dressed in goat, sheep, camel, and donkey costumes to characterize the live nativity scene. While the children sang hymns, a teenage girl and boy entered a stage door dressed in the ancient garb of Mary and Joseph holding the baby, and stood in front of the manger. Pastor and Mrs. Palmer's three-month-old baby represented the baby Jesus in Mary's arms. Some of the songs the children sang were the ones Christopher played the night before, along with "Away in a Manger", "O Holy Night", "God Rest Ye Merry Gentlemen", and "Hark the Herald Angels Sing". However, Jerilyn's biggest surprise occurred when Lily stepped forward from the front row, and she was handed a microphone. Jerilyn looked at Christopher, raised her eyebrow in question, and he just nodded. Out of that small child rang out the sweetest voice for "O Little Town of Bethlehem", Lily's favorite hymn. When Lily finished, she bowed and received a standing ovation, and Christopher and Jerilyn clapped the hardest. Jerilyn knew Lily would sing in the choir, but she wasn't told Lily would have a solo. "Lily's amazing, Christopher. You must be so proud."

"I am. Not because of her talent thought, she's just an all-around amazing kid. I have been blessed."

"Yes, you have."

When they neared the end of the program, Pastor Palmer walked out on stage. "I thank all of you for joining us tonight. I hope you have enjoyed our children's Christmas concert. Please stand and join the children for the final hymn "Silent Night".

The congregation and children's voices sang in reverent praise to the Lord, and Jerilyn had to take out her handkerchief to dab at her eyes. When she looked around, she saw Mrs. Bazell and many others in the congregation doing the same. *O dear Lord, I have missed You so!* She prayed in her heart. *Please help me decide my future.*

Chapter Thirteen

All Things Are Possible With God

"Fear thou not; for I am with thee: be not dismayed; for I am thy God: I will strengthen thee; yea, I will help thee; yea, I will uphold thee with the right hand of my righteousness."
Isaiah 41:10

Sunday evening
December 21, 1941
After lunch, Jerilyn exhausted herself playing in the snow with Christopher and Lily. At four o'clock she retired to her room to take a shower, change into dry clothes, and nap. When she awakened, she noticed it was almost time for dinner. She met the Bazells in the dining room.

Tired from all the activities of the day, Jerilyn knew the Bazells must be wondering why she was quiet and not very conversational, but she was still not ready to tell them about the pregnancy. Last night, she had asked Christopher to keep the information to himself for now, and he agreed.

After dinner, she returned to her room, sat in

the chair by the window, and picked up the Bible in her room. She opened it near the center and found Proverbs. At Proverbs 3:5-6 she paused. *Trust in the Lord with all thine heart; and lean not unto thine own understanding. In all thy ways acknowledge him, and he shall direct thy paths.*

She sat back and reflected on her life. She had not trusted in the Lord for any of her decisions. When she became a Christian, although young, she remembered being very happy. Her parents had raised her for that moment. She wanted Ken to be her boyfriend, but never consulted the Lord. Of course, she wasn't sorry she courted and married Ken, and was now extremely relieved he'd become a Christian before his death. She remembered the chapel downstairs. All seemed quiet in the hotel. Most of the guests had retired to their rooms, so she decided to go down to the chapel to pray.

She crept down the steps into the lobby. The night clerk on duty waved to her and she returned his wave. She entered the beautiful little chapel and looked straight ahead to the wooden cross before walking to the front pew and taking a seat. She sat and thought about the cross.

Her Lord and Savior had died so she might live, on a cross that was now empty, for Jesus had overcome death on that glorious first Easter Day. She stood and walked to the front and knelt on the steps that represented the altar in the chapel. In anguish she began to pray aloud. "*Dear Heavenly Father, I want to do Your will. I don't know the direction for my life that You want me to take. Please help me to be clear. I feel so confused. I loved Ken so much. Christopher has asked to court me. I've grown very fond of him and Lily. I don't want to be disloyal to Ken. How is it possible for me to love one man so much and then care about another in the same month? Dear Lord, please help me.*"

She began to cry softly.

A light hand touched her shoulder. She turned and saw Mrs. Bazell, who with the aid of her cane lowered herself onto her knees on the steps beside her. She looked at Jerilyn in such a kind and loving way. Through her blurry eyes, Jerilyn looked into the faded old blue eyes.

"My dear child, please do not think I'm intruding. I want to help you. I saw you come in here, and I see the distress that surrounds you. I noticed how quiet you were at dinner, and my heart goes out to you. Is there something I can do?"

Jerilyn answered tearfully, "Mrs. Bazell, I told you my husband Ken died at Pearl Harbor, but I didn't tell you I'm going to have his baby." She rubbed her stomach.

Mrs. Bazell reached in her pocket, withdrew a

handkerchief, and handed it to Jerilyn. Jerilyn accepted it with a smile. She blew her nose and looked back into the wrinkled and compassionate face.

"Why don't we have a seat on the pew?" suggested Mrs. Bazell. "My old bones can't kneel so long anymore."

Jerilyn helped Mrs. Bazell stand and they sat on the front pew. Mrs. Bazell took Jerilyn's hand. "A baby is a gift from God. He would not have given you this wonderful gift without a plan for your future."

"It's not just the baby. I loved my husband very much. In fact I've loved him since I met him when I was just fourteen years old. We married two years ago, six months after we graduated high school. I held his memorial service only nine days ago. We're only twenty years old, and now ... he's dead.

"Here I am at Christmas Hotel in Franklin, Kentucky, and I meant to travel to Nashville. Presently, I have no desire to continue on to Nashville nor to return home. In the short time I've been here, I've fallen in love with the mission of this hotel, with you, Captain Bazell, with Lily ... and I think I'm falling in love with Christopher. How can I possibly love two men at the same time? I'm not a wanton woman. I'm so confused." She hung her head in misery.

"Please do not weep, child. You are a young woman faced with difficulties that you did not anticipate. I believe the Lord has His hand on you. I do not think that it is a coincidence that you arrived at Christmas Hotel. I think the Lord planned for you to come here. The Lord may have meant for you to fall in love with Christopher and Lily. You are not a wanton woman to love two men. Ken was your past and Christopher may be your future. He is a wonderful father to Lily and would be to your baby, too. He was a wonderful husband to Ellie and would be for you. You do not have to love them the same. It will be different, but I feel certain you will have the Lord's blessing and you will be happy. You must pray about this. Has Christopher made his feelings known to you?"

"He told me he wishes to court me when I'm ready. How can a newly widowed woman with child possibly be ready to be courted?"

"All things are possible with God," Mrs. Bazell answered.

Jerilyn looked at her in surprise. "That's what Christopher and Lily said ... *and* Carrie Emeline."

It was Mrs. Bazell's turn to express surprise, but she responded in the same soft tone Jerilyn had used. "How do you know about Carrie Emeline?"

"That's an unbelievable story. Maybe we should go into the lobby in case someone needs to pray in the chapel tonight."

They settled on the sofa facing the Nativity scene. It was Jerilyn's turn to comfort, and she took the hand of Mrs. Bazell. "I know now why room number seven was never used. In fact, it has not been used for a great many years ... am I correct?"

"Yes, you are correct. That was the room our precious daughter Carrie Emeline lived in while she was here at Christmas Hotel."

"I know," Jerilyn responded with compassion. "I must tell you I found her diary from 1883 in my room."

Mrs. Bazell gasped. "I looked for the diary many times and never found it. Carrie Emeline began writing diaries from around the age of five. Early on, the diary was how she practiced printing her letters. I have every year through 1882, and 1884, but I was missing 1883. I am anxious to see what she wrote. If you have read it, then you know it was a tragic year for Carrie Emeline."

Jerilyn nodded; relieved to know she had done nothing wrong in reading it. "I will return it to you as soon as I go back upstairs. Yes, I did read her diary and it is for that reason that I rededicated my life to our Lord and Savior Jesus Christ. I was saved many years ago, but I drifted. Carrie Emeline's experience in 1883 helped me return to Him. Much of what happened to her has happened to me. The only difference in our situations was that she wasn't married to Seth. He didn't leave her a widow with child, but she was just as broken and depressed as I was.

"When you and Captain Bazell brought her to Christmas Hotel, she wrote that her depression began to lift ... as did mine. She states she rededicated her life to the Lord, and her life changed. She and I both found our miracle at Christmas Hotel. Mrs. Bazell, the blessing of the Lord is definitely on this hotel. I think she and I looked inward and found the Holy Spirit Who had never left us. It was Carrie Emeline and I who left *Him*. We both forgot to lean on Him. Yes, all things are possible with God."

"You are right, Jerilyn." Mrs. Bazell looked at the tree. "That tree is beautiful and so are the presents underneath, but it is not what is under the tree that is Christmas. It is the Holy Spirit living within us."

She turned to the Nativity scene. "Can you imagine being Mary ... the mother of our Lord? She carried Jesus in her womb and birthed Him. Every day on God's earth someone is being reborn. Someone is receiving the Holy Spirit. Jesus is born every day in someone's heart. That is why Christmas Hotel celebrates Christmas every day of the year. We must never forget the birth of Christ, and why He came here to die upon the cross. His plan was to save us from our sins, so we could live with Him forever. Can you imagine such love? He has brought you here, Jerilyn, as we brought Carrie Emeline. This is your next journey in life. You can grasp onto it with all your might, or you can reject it. The decision is yours to make for yourself, and for your baby.

"It was meant for Mary and Joseph to stay in a stable because all the rooms were filled at the inn. It was meant for you to stay in Carrie Emeline's room because all the rooms were filled at Christmas Hotel. You were the one meant to find that diary, all these years later. That is why I never found it."

"What happened to Carrie Emeline? The diary ended on December thirty-first, 1883."

"Our daughter did not live long into 1884. She died on March twentieth of that year from pneumonia. However, she died happy. She knew her Lord awaited her and she would see Seth again. I am sure she is probably wondering what is taking her father and me so long to join her!" she said, with a whimsical smile and the ever-present twinkle in her eyes. "Captain Bazell is now one hundred years old, and I am ninety-eight. Only the Lord knows why we have been kept here so long. I suppose we have not as yet fulfilled all our purposes. One does not know how long one's life will be. That is why it is so important to ask the Lord for salvation as soon as He knocks. It is never wise to wait. Carrie Emeline was less than a month shy of her twenty-second birthday when she died. I thank God she was a Christian."

"Where is Carrie Emeline buried?"

"She is here in Franklin at Greenlawn Cemetery. By the way, so are Christopher's parents, and his wife Ellie."

"I'm glad your daughter's grave is close for you and Captain Bazell. We know her spirit is with the Lord, but it's nice to visit and remember. Thank you for speaking with me, Mrs. Bazell. I can't tell you how much comfort you have brought me. I will pray about this."

The two women embraced and retired to their rooms.

As soon as Jerilyn entered her room, she remembered she had promised to return the diary. She opened the secret drawer, pulled out the diary, and hurried to Captain and Mrs. Bazell's room. Mrs. Bazell glanced inside the front cover, saw Carrie Emeline's handwriting, and hugged the little book to her breast. "Thank you, Jerilyn.".

The two women again said goodnight.

Jerilyn knelt beside her bed and prayed verbally. "*Dear Heavenly Father, thank You for loving me enough to send me to Christmas Hotel. I never thought I would ever thank someone for stealing my purse, but I do. I see now that all these events since I boarded the train in Dayton were planned by You. I will listen to Mrs. Bazell and seek this new journey in my life. When You see Ken, please tell him I love him. I will let our baby know him through my memories, and my baby will know he gave him or her life. Ken will always have a place in my heart. Tell Ken I thank him for leaving a part of himself with me. If it is Your will for me to court Christopher, please let me know for certain. In the name of Jesus I pray ... Amen."*

Chapter Fourteen

The New Arrivals

"But the path of the just is as the shining light, that shineth more and more unto the perfect day."
Proverb 4:18

Monday
December 22, 1941
Monday morning at the diner was much the same as usual. Christopher and Lily arrived at six o'clock while it was still dark, as did Jerilyn. Nettie Sue's fiancée showed up early that morning. He normally did not arrive until all his ice deliveries were complete, and this was the first time Jerilyn had spoken with him. Nettie Sue asked Jerilyn to come over to her station.

"Jerilyn, I'd like you to meet my fiancé Booker. Actually his name is James, but everyone calls him Booker. He leaves tomorrow to join the war."

Booker and Jerilyn shook hands, Jerilyn wished him well, and returned to her customers. Nettie Sue returned to Booker. Having no other customers, she stood in front of Booker, elbows on the counter and her chin in her hands, hanging on his every word. Jerilyn could see they were very much in love. They looked like she and Ken had when they were courting. The relationship with Christopher was so different. They each had been married, and he had a child and she would have one in May. If she and Christopher did court, it would certainly be unlike their first courtships.

Shortly before Jerilyn was ready to finish work, she looked at the next guests at her counter and blinked to make sure it wasn't her imagination. There sat her parents and her best friend Emma, along with Emma's husband Jack. Jerilyn ran around to their side and hugged each one.

"Oh, I can't believe you're here! I'm so pleased to see all of you!" She called over to Nettie Sue. "Nettie Sue, come over and meet my parents and my very best friends." Jerilyn introduced all of them. "Let me just finish a few of my side duties and we can walk to Christmas Hotel. I can't wait to show it to you."

On the way to the hotel she showed them the town, and pointed out places where she would take them later. "How long can you stay?" she asked.

Her mother replied happily. "None of us need to return to work until January fifth, so we can enjoy you, and all the things you wrote about in your letter."

They reached the hotel, and Emma was the first to respond. She looked up and down the exterior. "Wow! This is amazing."

Jerilyn touched Emma's arm. "Wait until you see the interior."

They entered the hotel and Jerilyn noted all their expressions of awe. She watched them take in the beauty of the hotel, much like she had on her first day here. She turned to the desk and saw Christopher watching them. She waved him over. "Christopher, I'd like to introduce you to my parents William and Evelyn Morgan, my best friend Emma, and her husband Jack Showalter."

They all shook hands. Mr. Morgan turned to Christopher. "I guess we need two rooms. I hope there's availability. I should have phoned."

"You're fine, sir. Due to two cancellations, there is availability tonight and tomorrow, but Wednesday is Christmas Eve and we're booked through New Year's Day," said Christopher. "How long are you staying?"

Jerilyn answered for her parents and friends. "They're staying past the New Year. They don't need to return to work until January fifth."

Christopher's face brightened. "Jerilyn, why not have all of them spend two nights here to relish the atmosphere of Christmas Hotel, and the remainder of the week at my home. I have plenty of room with three spare bedrooms."

"Oh, we don't want to impose," Mrs. Morgan said quickly.

"Ma'am, it's no imposition. Jerilyn's family and friends are most welcome. Please do me the honor of hosting you."

Mr. Morgan answered for the four of them. "Well, if it's no imposition, we'd be delighted."

Christopher checked them in and had the bellhop carry the bags to their rooms on the fourth floor. Jerilyn told them to unpack and rest, and she would seat them in the dining room at six o'clock. To Christopher she mouthed, "Thank you."

He returned with a, "You're welcome."

Later that evening, Jerilyn introduced her parents and friends to the Bazells, before seating them in the dining room. While she worked, she tried to go to their table to spend some time with them. They understood and waved her off to her job.

"Don't apologize," her father said. "I understand you have your duties. Don't worry about us. Go ahead and greet your guests."

She was exhausted when she finished her shift, but headed to the fourth floor to say goodnight to her parents and friends. Christopher had managed to place them in rooms that were side-by-side. Jerilyn said she would meet them in the lobby at five forty-five in the morning, so they could walk with her to Mr. Blakeley's diner in the train station for breakfast.

"Get a good night's sleep, and I'll see all of you in the morning. I'm so happy you're all here. It would not seem like Christmas without all of you."

Her mom kissed her cheek. "We felt the same way, too, dear. Sleep well and we'll see you in the morning."

Jerilyn knelt by the bed in her room. "Thank you, Lord. My parents and best friends arriving at Christmas Hotel was certainly an unexpected and surprise blessing. Thank You for this early Christmas gift. You never cease to amaze me."

Chapter Fifteen

Lily

"Be strong and of a good courage, fear not,
nor be afraid of them: for the Lord thy God,
he it is that doth go with thee;
he will not fail thee, nor forsake thee."
Deuteronomy 31:6

Tuesday morning
December 23, 1941
The next morning, Jerilyn, her parents, Emma, and Jack arrived at the diner at the same time as Christopher and Lily. Nearly all the snow had melted and the thermometer on the outside wall registered above freezing. They hung their coats on the hooks, and all six sat at Jerilyn's row of stools. Jerilyn tied on her apron and introduced Lily to her parents and friends,

"Lily, I'd like you to meet my parents, Mr. and Mrs. Morgan."

Lily jumped off her stool, and with a slight curtsy said, "Hello, Mr. and Mrs. Morgan."

Jerilyn's parents responded with a smile, and

said, "Hello, to you Miss Lily. How are you?"

"I'm fine."

When introduced to Emma and Jack, she curtsied again, and echoed the hello again.

Emma whispered to Jack, "What a sweet, precocious little girl."

Lily's ears perked up. "What's precocious, Daddy?"

Chuckles sounded all over the diner.

Christopher hugged Lily. "They think you are mature for your age, honey." Lily beamed and took her seat back upon the stool.

Christopher said he had asked Mrs. Evans to meet them here at the diner, pick up Lily, and give Jerilyn's family and friends the tour of Franklin, while Jerilyn was at work. After work, Jerilyn would give them the tour of Christmas Hotel.

After Jerilyn completed her lunch shift, she returned to Christmas Hotel to meet up with her parents and friends. She stopped at the front desk for a friendly chat with Christopher.

Christopher glanced towards the staircase and Jerilyn noticed the sudden embarrassment on his face. She turned and saw her parents, Emma and Jack, and the Bazells all watching – and appearing pleased. She blushed, managed to speak, but stumbled in her words. "Are ... are you all ready for the tour of Christmas Hotel?" she asked them.

Smiling, they all replied with a resounding "Yes!"

She gave them the same guided tour Christopher had given to her last week. When she came to the crates marked CEB, she told them the story about finding the diary and reading it. When she reached the part about Carrie Emeline rededicating her life to the Lord, she lowered her head, and said softly, "So I did, too."

"Oh, Jerilyn!" her mother said happily. "This *is* an answer to prayer!" She hugged Jerilyn, and then handed her off to her father and friends for more hugs. The three women pulled out their handkerchiefs and dabbed their eyes. "We are such crybabies," her Mom said while still dabbing her eyes.

At last Jerilyn was free to speak without crying. "I have so much to tell you, that I hardly know where to begin. Why don't we go to my room? I can begin there."

Jerilyn spent the remainder of the afternoon relaying the events of the previous week. "I felt a kinship with Carrie Emeline. She loved her Seth so much, as I loved my Ken," she said quietly. "However, Carrie Emeline was much closer to the Lord than I was. Although we were both saved at a young age, she continued to serve the Lord, and I simply did not. We both went through depression when our men died, but we both found comfort and our miracle in this blessed hotel. We both rededicated our lives shortly after coming here. I feel as if the Lord drew me to this place, just as the Bazells were drawn here to help their daughter. The Lord gave us peace when we placed our trust in Him." She stopped a moment, closed her eyes in thought, reopened them and continued.

"Captain and Mrs. Bazell are amazing people. They're actually the second proprietors of this hotel. Thomas Hoy built this hotel in 1850 and sold it to the Bazells late in 1883. The mission plan was for people to understand that the birth of Jesus should be celebrated every day and not just on one day. Only He could save us from our sins, not us. The Bazells kept the mission of the hotel. That's why Christmas is celebrated every day at Christmas Hotel. The chapel downstairs has served for many weddings. It also has a portable baptistery tank, deep enough to cover someone fully. Many people have been baptized here in the winter months, when it's been too cold to go to one of the creeks."

Jerilyn's father looked at his watch. "It's five o'clock. Are you working this evening, Jerilyn?"

"Actually, no. The Bazells offered to give me the night off. Christopher has invited us all to dinner at his home at six o'clock. Mrs. Evans is cooking and she's a wonderful cook."

"Oh, you've eaten there before?" Emma asked, with an impish grin.

Jerilyn blushed, but managed to say, "Yes, I have."

They stared at her, and she knew they wanted to hear more. She remembered their expressions when they saw her in the lobby with Christopher. With a big sigh she began. "I suppose you want to hear about Christopher and Lily."

"It's about time," Emma said with her hands on her hips for emphasis.

Jerilyn shook her head. "Emma, you don't mess around when you want information. Okay, here's the scoop. He's a widower." She went on to tell them the story of Christopher entering the army air corps, serving as the chaplain, and meeting and marrying Ellie. She told of the tragic death of Ellie giving birth to Lily on Easter Sunday, 1936. "You'd think Christopher would be bitter, but he's not. He loves the Lord, and he's raising Lily to love the Lord, too."

A knock on the door interrupted their conversation. Jerilyn opened it to Mrs. Bazell. "You must come quickly, Jerilyn. Mrs. Evans is in the lobby. She says Lily has been hit by a car and Christopher needs you."

Jerilyn turned to her family and felt the blood draining from her face.

"Go to him," her father said. "We'll go down to the chapel and pray for Lily and Christopher ... and for you."

Mrs. Evans filled Jerilyn in on the details of the accident as they hurried to Christopher's house. Lily had been playing with her friend Ruth in front of Ruth's house, across the street on South College Street. They were playing a variation of the schoolyard game Four-square, called Sidewalk Two-square. The ball rolled into the street and Lily stepped off the curb to retrieve it. Ruth's mother said she was watching them out her window, and ran to the door to tell Lily to stop. The driver of a car coming down the street did not see Lily until it was too late. The front fender hit Lily, pitching her little body onto the sidewalk.

Ruth screamed, which sent Mrs. Evans and other neighbors to their doors. Christopher was in his room dressing for dinner. Mrs. Evans yelled for him to come and hurry, and then she ran to the street. Lily was not moving, and blood flowed from a wound on her head. Mrs. Evans described to Jerilyn how she knelt down, opened Lily's coat, and placed her ear on Lily's heart. She then felt Lily's wrist for her pulse. She heard and felt Lily breathing, but barely. She stepped out of her petticoat and wrapped it around Lily's head, tying it securely.

Ruth's mother had then asked a neighbor boy to hurry and fetch Dr. Beasley. The boy took off running as fast as his legs would carry him. The woman who had been driving the car stood nearby and cried hysterically. She kept saying "I'm so sorry," over and over.

Mrs. Evans said Christopher ran to his daughter and fell to his knees. "Someone bring me two blankets, please," he shouted.

Ruth's mother hurried into the house and returned with the blankets. Christopher maneuvered one blanket under Lily and covered her with the other to await Dr. Beasley. He was afraid to pick her up and carry her to the house for fear of causing further injuries.

He then turned to Mrs. Evans. "Please go get Jerilyn. Tell her ... I need her," he choked.

Mrs. Evans said the last sound she heard before leaving was Christopher praying over his unconscious daughter.

When Jerilyn and Mrs. Evans approached Christopher's house, they saw that Dr. Beasley had arrived in his Ford woody wagon. Mrs. Evans told Jerilyn he normally didn't drive that particular vehicle unless he was transporting a patient to Protestant Hospital in Nashville, so things appeared serious.

They stood close and watched Dr. Beasley check

Lily's breathing with his stethoscope. She was still unconscious. He examined the head wound and felt over her body, checking for broken bones. He cleaned the head wound and covered it with a moist gauze, followed by an application of dry gauze before he covered the wound with a bandage. "I must commend the person who thought to wrap this child's head with the petticoat. Initially, it did slow the bleeding."

"That would be Mrs. Evans," said Christopher.

"That was quick thinking," Dr. Beasley said to Mrs. Evans.

Mrs. Evans attempted a smile. "Thank you, Dr. Beasley."

Dr. Beasley finished his evaluation and turned to Christopher. "She remains unconscious, and I believe her shoulder is broken. I don't know if she has any internal injuries. I could set her shoulder now, but I don't want to take the time. The head wound is the most important, and time is of the essence. I think we should drive her to Protestant Hospital in Nashville immediately. I brought my neighbor's son Jim to do the driving in anticipation of this. I have the back of my wagon laid down, and I will ride in the back with Lily to monitor her breathing. You can ride in the front with Jim."

"May I go, too?" Jerilyn asked.

"Is there room up front for three?" asked

Christopher.

Jim answered for Dr. Beasley. "There's plenty of room. Let's go."

"Jerilyn, I will take care of your family's move in the morning if you're not home," said Mrs. Evans.

"I completely forgot about them. Thank you, Mrs. Evans. I appreciate your help."

"It's not a problem, dear. We'll all be praying from here."

Jim and Christopher picked up the sides of the blanket under Lily and carried her to the automobile in the fading light, while Jerilyn opened the front door and scooted over to the middle. Dr. Beasley hopped in the back of the station wagon with Lily leaving the other blanket on top of her. Christopher ran back into the house for his pocket Bible, then he and Jim jumped in, closed the doors, and they were off.

The road to Nashville was crowded with Christmas travelers. Christopher explained he had often driven the forty-five miles on the two-lane road in just over an hour. With the traffic, it would probably take at least thirty minutes longer. Jerilyn thought Jim was doing a tremendous job missing the potholes, and passing the slower drivers, too. At least it was dinner time, and now almost dark, so no slow-moving tractors clogged the road.

They pulled in front of the hospital, Dr. Beasley

explained the emergency, and the staff moved Lily to a gurney and whisked her away. Jerilyn followed closely with Christopher and Dr. Beasley, while Jim parked the station wagon in the doctors' lot.

Lily, along with Dr. Beasley, was taken into the examination room, while Christopher and Jerilyn were asked to stay in the waiting room.

Christopher and Jerilyn sat side-by-side, holding hands and praying. After about fifteen minutes they leaned back in their chairs and watched the clock. They kept silent, lost in their own thoughts. Christopher turned to Jerilyn and again took her hand. "Thank you for being here with me. It means a lot."

"Christopher, there's no other place I would want to be. I've grown to love Lily. Oh, Christopher," she choked, and began to cry, "I'm sorry. I wasn't going to do this." She removed a handkerchief from her pocket. "I'm sorry. I was going to be so strong for you."

"It's all right, Jerilyn." Christopher placed his arm around her. "I just need someone with me that cares ... for us." He paused, and said, "She was so small lying in the street."

"She's alive, Christopher. That's what we need to hold on to."

It had now been one hour since Lily went into the examining room. An aid approached, asking if there was anything she could get them. They thanked her and said they were fine. Fifteen minutes later, Dr. Beasley walked into the waiting room and they both stood as he approached.

"I'm sorry ..."

Jerilyn felt her heart leap in panic.

Dr. Beasley coughed. "Excuse me. I didn't mean to scare you. I'm sorry it's been such a long wait for you. I wanted to give the doctors as much information as I could and tell them what we had already done. They are still running some of the preliminary tests on Lily's head. While that was being done, we set her shoulder. There should be no permanent damage there. I don't think the car was going that fast. If she hadn't hit her head on the sidewalk, I could have set her shoulder and we wouldn't be here right now. It's Lily's head that concerns me, along with the unconsciousness. There's a head trauma specialist in with her right now."

Jim walked up. "I've been here for a while," he said softly. "I just didn't want to interrupt you two with your prayers and comfort of each other. Please know I'm praying for your little girl, too."

"Thank you," Christopher said.

Jerilyn noticed Jim said it as if they were both Lily's parents. "Dr. Beasley, what's the next step?" she asked.

"I'm waiting for the specialist to finish his evaluation. I don't think he'll be much longer."

No sooner did he get the words out when a doctor came out of Lily's room and walked up to Christopher and Jerilyn. "Hello, my name is Dr. Rouse." He shook hands with Christopher. "I suppose you two are the little girl's parents?"

Christopher looked at Jerilyn and said, "I'm her father."

"Well, please allow me to brief you as simply as possible. Your little girl has a brain trauma."

Jerilyn observed Christopher wince.

"Brain traumas come in different stages," Dr. Rouse continued. "We're trying to find out how severe Lily's is and what the complications might be. Basically, she has experienced a blunt force trauma. Let me explain. The cerebral cortex, which is the gray matter, can become bruised. If the force is severe enough, a whiplash can occur to the nerve cells deep in the white matter of the brain. The cranium is the structure of bones protecting the brain. It has three layers and when a blunt object, such as the pavement, comes in contact with the bones of the skull, several reactions are possible. Sometimes a piece of bone can break loose from the skull and is forced into the cranium. Sometimes the object bends the skull inward. Sometimes the skull is bent inward and outward, that causes radiating fractures from the impact site.

"Even if the skull is not penetrated, when a moving head comes to a quick stop, as when her head hit the pavement, the brain continues in its movement, striking the interior of the skull. This can cause bruising of the brain or a contusion and bleeding or hemorrhage. In cases of blunt head trauma, the brain can also be injured directly opposite the site of trauma – on the other side of the brain."

A sudden thought occurred to Jerilyn, a silly one considering the desperate situation. "Her hair. Have you ...?"

Dr. Rouse seemed relieved to change to more mundane matters. "It will regrow quickly," he said. "It was necessary to shave her head for our inspection, and to keep the wound clean. There was grit in the wound from the street."

Jerilyn realized she should be much less interested in the loss of Lily's curls than in her survival. "So what is your diagnosis?"

"We are currently looking for edema, which is a swelling of the brain, and hematoma which is a collection of blood due to tissue injury or the tearing of a blood vessel, or a collection of fluid in and around the brain. If any of this occurs, there will be necessary steps to take. Her vitals are stable, and she's still comatose. I'm afraid it's going to be a long night. You may want to check into a hotel and we can call you if there is any change."

Christopher answered in a firm voice. "I won't be going anywhere, Dr. Rouse, but thank you for the suggestion. I will be right here when you know anything. Please let me know immediately if there's any change. Is there any possibility that we can see her now?"

Dr. Rouse seemed to be mulling the situation over. "I don't think there will be any harm in that. Just give me thirty minutes, and I'll allow you and your wife to come into the room."

"Thank you, doctor." Christopher patted Jerilyn's hand, while Dr. Rouse returned to Lily's room. Addressing Dr. Beasley and Jim, Christopher said, "I see no reason for you two to stay here any longer. I will call you when there's a change in Lily's status. Jerilyn, you should go with them. You have family at home."

"Christopher, I don't want to leave. Please let me stay with you and Lily. My family will be fine with Mrs. Evans."

He looked into her eyes. "Thank you, Jerilyn. I would very much appreciate your company."

Christopher turned back to Dr. Beasley and Jim. "Dr. Beasley, thank you very much. Thank you, too, Jim for getting us safely to the hospital."

"You're welcome, Christopher," said Dr.

Beasley.

The two men turned, leaving Christopher and Jerilyn alone and scared.

Chapter Sixteen

The Long Night

"Blessed be God, even the Father of our Lord Jesus Christ, the Father of mercies, and the God of all comfort; who comforteth us in all our tribulation, that we may be able to comfort them which are in any trouble, by the comfort wherewith we ourselves are comforted of God."
2 Corinthians 1:3-4

Tuesday Evening, December 23
and Wednesday morning, December 24, 1941
True to his word, Dr. Rouse did allow them a brief visit with Lily. Because there was a concern for germs and infection, Christopher and Jerilyn had to scrub up and wear hospital gowns, gloves, and masks before entering. Christopher and Jerilyn stood inside the doorway taking in the scene with Lily. Two nurses stood quietly in the room. One was checking her vital signs and the other was adjusting the intravenous tube in her vein that was giving the little girl nourishment. She looked so small in the adult-size bed. Her face was as pale as the white

pillowcase on which her bandaged head rested. However, she seemed to be breathing steadily.

Jerilyn managed to stay calm as she stared at the bandages on Lily's head. Under those bandages would be a shaved scalp. It was almost too much to bear to think of all those lovely curls gone, but at least little Lily was alive.

She returned with Christopher to the waiting room. The wall clock said nine, and Jerilyn suggested it would be a good time to get a sandwich and some coffee. They left instructions with the head nurse where they would be if there was any change. They followed the signs to the hospital cafeteria which was open twenty-four hours a day. Selecting ham and cheese sandwiches, they took a table by the window away from the hospital personnel and other visitors.

Christopher held Jerilyn's hand and they bowed their heads to pray. As they raised their heads an old couple approached their table.

When the woman spoke, her mouth trembled and her voice wavered. "We're sorry to bother you, but we saw you praying. Are you a preacher?"

Christopher must have seen the anxiety on their faces. With kindness and compassion Christopher spoke to the old couple, "Presently I am not a preacher, but I have been."

Jerilyn noticed their deflated expression, and

desired with all her heart for Christopher to reach out to them. "Help them," she whispered.

He touched the old woman's hand. "How may I help?"

"Our eight-year-old grandson ... David ... is here. They say he has meningitis. The doctor told us to go and pray. There's not a whole lot they can do for him. He's currently in isolation ... and our son and daughter-in-law ... are not allowed into the room." The elderly woman struggled with her words and dabbed her eyes with her handkerchief.

Her husband continued for her. "There's a new drug they would like to try on David, but it has not been marketed and approved, as yet. Vanderbilt University Hospital has a small amount, but the drug has not been used in America. It has, however, been used in England with some success, and is currently being produced in small quantities in some American laboratories. It was only determined earlier this year that it's not toxic to humans. They call it penicillin. My son is uncertain what to do. We went to see the hospital chaplain to pray with us, but the chaplain is home sick tonight. My wife and I saw you two praying. My son needs to make a decision soon. Will you pray ... for us?" Now the old man's voice became shaky, too.

"I would be most happy to pray with you." Christopher jumped up, grabbed a couple of chairs and asked the old couple to sit with them. He took Jerilyn's hand and the old man's, while Jerilyn took the old woman's hand, and the old woman took her husband's hand, forming a circle. "What are your names?"

"We're Henry and Edna," the old man said.

They bowed their heads, and Christopher began to pray. "*Dear Heavenly Father, we come to You tonight to pray for David, who is Henry and Edna's grandson. David needs the healing touch of Jesus Christ Your precious Son. David's father needs Your help in deciding whether to permit the doctors to allow this new drug called penicillin to be used on his son. Please touch David's father and help him make the decision that is Your will. Please help Henry and Edna to know Your peace, as in 2 Corinthians 12: 9. 'And he said unto me, My grace is sufficient for thee: for my strength is made perfect in weakness. Most gladly therefore will I rather glory in my infirmities, that the power of Christ may rest upon me.' I thank You for sending Henry and Edna to Jerilyn and me to allow us to pray for David and his family. In the name of Your Son Jesus Christ we pray ... Amen.*"

The other three added their amens.

Henry wiped a tear from his eye. "Thank you, sir ... ma'am," as he looked to each of them. "Thank you for taking the time to pray with us. I haven't even asked *your* names."

"We are Jerilyn and Christopher," responded Christopher.

"Well, God bless you two and thank you again. I apologize for not asking you why you're here. Is it a family member?"

"Yes," answered Christopher. "She's my daughter, and she was hit by a car."

Henry shook his head. "I'm sorry to hear that. Edna and I will pray for her tonight every time we pray for David. What's your daughter's name?"

"Her name is Lily. I will appreciate your prayers ... and thank you. Please get word to me tonight at any time about David's condition. We'll be in the waiting room on the fourth floor."

The old couple rose, and Edna said, "Again, thank you, and God bless you and your wife."

"You're welcome," responded Christopher, without explaining to them that Jerilyn was not his wife.

Jerilyn could only smile at Henry and Edna.

****

At midnight, Jerilyn and Christopher were still awake. They sat at each end of the sofa in the waiting room, each covered by a blanket, with their heads resting on pillows an aid brought. No one else had been in the waiting room all night. They spent the time in prayer for Lily and David, while getting to know more about each other.

"You know, while I was praying for David and his family, for the first time since Lily's accident I didn't think about Lily," Christopher said. "It was like when I was a chaplain. I oftentimes thought of others before myself. Even before this happened, I've been feeling the nudge again. It's as if the Holy Spirit is saying, 'It's time.' I told you after Ellie died that I was depressed. Even when I returned to normal – or what I thought was normal – I didn't have that intense feeling I needed to preach. Before, when I was at the base, it was like a fire burning within me.

"Ellie and I arrived in Franklin three months before Lily was born. There are many small neighborhood churches in the area, but I'd not found a permanent home church as a preacher. In fact, I'd not done much work of any kind and had considered re-enlisting. I needed regular work to support my growing family.

"The week before Ellie went into premature labor, I preached on Palm Sunday at a little church twelve miles in the country called Mt. Vernon Missionary Baptist Church. They were looking for a permanent pastor. I promised them I'd return the following Sunday to preach the Easter service.

"The Mt. Vernon deacons held a meeting the Wednesday evening after I preached, and voted to ask me to be their permanent preacher. They drove into town the day before Easter to ask me. I told them I was honored, but I would need to pray about it and discuss it with Ellie. I figured if we took the position, we'd need to move closer to the church. Mr. Roy Harris, one of the deacons, said he had a tenant house for rent. He even said I could work for him on his farm during the week for extra money. By the way, he's Nettie Sue's dad."

Jerilyn nodded. "I met him once when he picked her up from work. Her fiancée Booker picks her up most of the time, but now he's in boot camp. Mr. Harris drops Nettie Sue off most mornings before I get there, so I normally don't get to see him."

Christopher seemed lost in his memories. "Late Saturday evening, Ellie didn't feel well, and she awakened early Sunday morning feeling worse. I called the home of another itinerant preacher who was available to preach the Easter Sunday service at Mt. Vernon. Although I knew Mrs. Evans would sit with Ellie, I didn't want to leave her and travel twelve miles out into the country.

"Well, as you know, Ellie gave birth two weeks prematurely and died. The last thing I wanted to do was preach. I told the deacons to look elsewhere. They heard the bitterness, and offered to pray with me. I wasn't interested. I was mad at God, but even after I atoned to God for my behavior, I no longer felt the call to preach. I could pray again as a normal Christian man, just not preach. The sermons no longer filled my head.

"Just recently, that seems to have changed. I've been hearing the small voice within me speak sermons again. When I'm reading the scriptures, they come alive in a message from God. I'm beginning to feel the call again. I must admit I like the feeling. I feel as if a part of me has been dead since Ellie died, and now it's awakening."

"Christopher, I'm happy for you. I understand what you mean, but in a completely different way. When I received the telegram that Ken was dead, a part of me died. Two weeks ago I would have thought I would never feel contentment again. You know when you prayed that scripture with Henry and Edna, 2 Corinthians 12: 9? That was the first scripture I read when I rededicated my life to the Lord on Thursday evening last week. I'd not lived for the Lord in many years. I did what I wanted to do. However, this is probably not a good time to tell you about that."

"I'd love to hear your testimony, Jerilyn. Now is a perfect time."

However, before she could begin, a nurse walked up to them. Behind her they watched Dr. Rouse enter Lily's room. Jerilyn was aware that Dr.

Rouse's presence was not a good sign, and noticed Christopher appeared anxious.

"I'm sorry to interrupt you," the nurse began. "We've called Dr. Rouse back in. Lily's head seems to have some swelling. It may be nothing. It's just a precaution. Dr. Rouse will talk to you as soon as he examines your daughter."

"Thank you, nurse," was all Christopher said.

Jerilyn took his hand. When the nurse walked away, together they prayed again for Lily.

Dr. Rouse stayed in Lily's room about thirty minutes, and then he walked out to Christopher and Jerilyn, and shook Christopher's hand with great sensitivity. "I'm seeing some swelling in Lily's brain. When I checked her pupils with the light, I could see a slight difference in equality than when she was first admitted. That may signify a rise in intracranial pressure. At this moment I'm going to have the nurses keep a close watch. They will be checking her eyes every fifteen minutes, along with her vitals. Please don't be alarmed. I can be here within fifteen minutes if the need for surgery should arise. Currently, Lily's vitals are steady."

Christopher thanked Dr. Rouse, and Dr. Rouse turned, walked to the elevator, and was gone.

Christopher stared after him, seeming to be deep in thought. Jerilyn touched his arm. She was trying her best to console Christopher, but knew she needed to console herself, too. She had come to love Lily. *God, please take care of Lily,* she prayed in her heart. Aloud she said, "Dr. Rouse told us not to be alarmed, Christopher. It may be nothing. I know they're being as careful as possible."

"I know. Thank you, Jerilyn."

They sat back down to watch more time pass by. According to the clock it was now two o'clock. They didn't say much for the next hour. They just held hands to pray.

At three o'clock Christopher spoke again. "I need to tell you something."

Jerilyn turned to him so he would know he had her full attention.

"After Lily was injured and I put the blankets over and under her, I began to pray. Dr. Beasley hadn't arrived, so it was just God and me. I heard the small voice say, 'If I take her to her heavenly home, will you still love and trust Me?' I ignored the voice and kept praying. It got louder. 'If I take her to her heavenly home, will you still love and trust Me?' I ignored it again, hoping the voice would go away. I denied what I thought I heard, and continued praying. All at once, I *could not* pray. I heard it again, louder than the first two times. 'If I take her to her heavenly home, will you still love and trust Me?' I knew I could no longer ignore the voice of God."

With a huge sigh, Christopher continued. "I answered Him, 'Yes, God, I will still love and trust You. If You take Lily home with You, I will not blame You as I did when Ellie died.' The words of my father-in-law rang in my ears. 'As long as there is sin in the world there will be situations none of us can control. We don't know why bad things happen to good people.' I was able to pray again, which I did until Dr. Beasley arrived. I'm not sure if God was testing me or not. I thought about the Bible story of Abraham and Isaac. Abraham almost killed his own son because he thought that's what God wanted him to do. God was only testing Abraham to see if he would obey Him in any situation."

They sat quietly for a while after that, both lost in thought. Jerilyn wondered if God was answering Lily's prayer for her Christmas wish – a mother. *Was He taking Lily home to Ellie? Was He testing Christopher's faith?*

At five o'clock Christopher asked, "Jerilyn, would you tell me about your salvation experience? I'd love to hear your testimony, *if* you feel so inclined to tell me."

"Of course. My parents were Christians and had been since they were children. I suppose I heard the hymns and the Gospels from the days in the womb. They were in church every time the doors were open. I grew up knowing the plan of salvation, but I didn't fall under conviction until I was eleven years old. One Sunday in church the message I'd heard all my life came alive. The preacher was preaching on Romans 3: 23, 'For all have sinned, and come short of the glory of God.'

"I'd memorized that scripture as a young child, but for the first time I realized I was a sinner. I realized I wouldn't get to heaven just because my parents were Christians. I knew I couldn't wait another day – I needed the Lord. I was completely under conviction, and the tears streamed down my face. My mother saw and knew what was happening. At the end of the Lord's message, the preacher and the congregation prayed for the unsaved and then began a hymn. I can't tell you which hymn, because I literally ran down that aisle.

"I wasn't sure what to do, and the preacher's wife prayed with me. I asked for her help and she opened her Bible. She asked me if I knew I was a sinner, and I said I was. She asked me if I knew I couldn't save myself with good works, but that only the grace of Jesus Christ could save me from my sins, as the Bible says in Romans 11: 6. I said I did. I knew Jesus Christ had come to earth to die on the cross, as the sacrificed Lamb of God to die in my place. She explained that God could not look upon sin, and everyone is born with the sinful nature.

Jesus Christ took my sin upon Himself and paid my sin debt in full, so I could dwell eternally with the Lord.

"She asked me if I knew John 3: 16, which I did. I recited it to her. 'For God so loved the world that he gave his only begotten Son, that whosoever believeth in him should not perish, but have everlasting life.' I told her that was the first verse I ever learned. However, that was the first time I recited it and knew what it meant. I realized God really loved me so much that He would have His Son die in my place to pay for my sins. She asked me if I believed Jesus was not dead, but had risen from the grave to take His eternal place beside His Father in Heaven.

"I said I did. She told me all I had to do was receive Him in my heart, which I did with joy. I felt the peace of the Lord fall all over me. The tears ran down my face again as she hugged me. It was late March, and as soon as the weather warmed I was baptized in the Great Miami River with several others from our church." Jerilyn stopped a moment to wipe a tear. "It's been a long time since I relived my salvation. Thank you for listening, Christopher."

"It's been a long time since I've heard the joy relived. As a chaplain, I watched people get saved and heard testimonies frequently. It does my heart good to hear the re-telling. As you gave your testimony, I again felt the call to preach. I know now that the Lord has been nudging me in that direction. I feel a peace, too. Thank *you,* Jerilyn."

Chapter Seventeen

The Long Day

"To every thing there is a season, and a time to every purpose under the heaven: A time to be born, and a time to die; a time to plant, and a time to pluck up that which is planted."
Ecclesiastes 3:1-2

Wednesday morning
December 24, 1941
At six-thirty, Jerilyn and Christopher asked the aid where they could get a couple of towels, washcloths, soap, toothbrushes, and toothpaste. The aid delivered the necessary items, and they spent the next thirty minutes freshening in the waiting room restrooms. They exited the two restrooms about the same time.

Jerilyn noticed that, like her, Christopher had wrapped his toothbrush and soap in tissue, anticipating the possibility of using them another day. She put hers and Christopher's into her purse.

At seven o'clock the shift change occurred and Dr. Rouse entered Lily's room at seven-thirty. He was only in there a few minutes. He walked over to Christopher and Jerilyn who were already on their feet with hopeful anticipation.

"I'm sorry," said Dr. Rouse. "There's no change in the swelling, except now Lily's running a minor fever and her blood pressure is a little elevated. Lily will continue to be monitored every fifteen minutes. I do have two surgeries this morning, but I plan to be available all day. The nurses are busy right now, but they can let you in the room to see Lily for a few minutes after nine."

Christopher thanked him, and as if in a daze they watched Dr. Rouse step onto the elevator.

Christopher turned to Jerilyn. "This doesn't sound good."

"Dr. Rouse only said minor," Jerilyn said encouragingly, not only to Christopher, but for her own benefit as well. "It may be that Lily's body is just working hard to fight back."

"Let's get off this floor for a while," said Christopher. "Some breakfast and more coffee in the cafeteria sound good about now. I know my legs are cramped from sitting on the sofa all night, and I expect that yours are, too."

They reported to the nurses' station to explain where they would be, if any change occurred.

The lines were longer this time. "All the visitors and hospital personnel must be eating breakfast at the same time," Christopher said half-jokingly.

They barely had enough time to receive the food, eat it, and return to the waiting area by nine. They didn't want to miss the chance to visit Lily as soon as they were permitted.

It was a few minutes past nine when they returned to the fourth floor. They checked in at the nurses' station and were told they could visit as soon as they scrubbed up, donned the hospital gowns, gloves, and masks. Ten minutes later they were in Lily's room.

She looked the same as she had last night, just as pale, and just as still. They watched the IV liquids as they entered her little arm, as one nurse took her vitals. Christopher asked about her blood pressure, and was told it was still elevated. Lily still had a minor fever and her pulse was somewhat rapid.

"Her pulse is rapid? Dr. Rouse didn't tell us that," Christopher said, almost in disbelief.

"I'm sorry," the nurse said with sympathy. "That just happened in the last hour."

"Does Dr. Rouse know?"

"We called the surgery to report. He told us to call back if it gets worse. I'm sorry, but I can't let you stay in here more than a few minutes. Dr. Rouse will be back within three hours, and I'll try to get you back in Lily's room shortly after."

At ten o'clock an aid came by to tell them they had a long distance call at the nurses' station. They hurried to the phone and Christopher took the receiver. "Hello. Mrs. Evans? Yes, we stayed in the waiting room all night. Yes ... well ... her shoulder was broken and that's been set, but she's still comatose. Also, there's some swelling in her brain."

Jerilyn could only hear Christopher's half of the conversation, but she could tell Mrs. Evans was peppering him with questions.

"No, they're not talking surgery at this time. Well, yes, there's more." He took a deep breath. "Her blood pressure and pulse are a little high and she's running some temperature ... Well, they're keeping a constant watch on her, and keeping us well informed ... Yes, they have let us in twice to see her. We're expecting to be allowed in again this afternoon ... Yes, I'll tell her that Ruth misses her ... All right, I'll call you if there's any change ... She's right here. I'll put her on."

Christopher handed Jerilyn the phone, and whispered, "Your father wants to speak with you."

"Hello, Dad ... Oh, that's good, I'm glad you're all moved into Christopher's house. Please tell Mrs. Evans thank you for me ... Yes, I'm going to be here for a while. I want to make certain Lily is out of danger ... You're right, the Bazells are sweet people. Please tell them thank you, and we appreciate their prayers. We appreciate all your prayers, too ... Thank you. I'll tell him. Goodbye."

"Tell me what?" Christopher asked.

"He said to tell you that people from all over Franklin have been dropping in with food dishes, and wishing you and Lily well. You and Lily are on every prayer chain in all of Simpson County."

At that, Christopher hung his head and cried for the first time.

Jerilyn took his arm and guided him back to the sofa. She put her arms around him and let him cry on her shoulder. She could not hold back any longer and began to cry, too. They held each other supportively until the tears were gone.

When they finally broke apart, they reached for their handkerchiefs. Between sniffles and blowing his nose, Christopher managed to say, "That's my community. They did the same when Ellie died. That's just the way those good people are. The visitation and funeral for my parents were huge, and just about everyone in Simpson County, Kentucky, was there."

They took their seats back on the sofa.

"I'd love to hear about your parents," she said quietly. "If now isn't a good time, we can talk another time."

"No, I'd like to tell you the story, and it will take my mind off Lily for a while. I had some pretty terrific parents growing up. I only wish they'd had more children. I missed not having a brother or a sister. My parents were quiet people. We went to church as a family, we read books, and listened to the radio. Dad taught history at Franklin High School. Mom liked to sing and play the piano. Over the years, she had quite a few students coming to the house for lessons. She taught me. She played the organ at church and sang. So I suppose you could say both of my parents were teachers.

"They were so excited the Friday morning they drove off for their second honeymoon. It was mid-October, 1930, and Dad had secured lodging at *LeConte Lodge* atop Mount LeConte in the Smoky Mountains of Tennessee. He said they'd be there at just the right time for the beautiful autumn colors, and he scared Mom a little when he added, 'along with viewing a few black bears.'"

Christopher looked at Jerilyn and winked.

"I think I could have lived without the black bears, too!" she said.

"I still have the one postcard they sent home. It said the usual: *Son, having a great time. Wish you were here. We'll be home soon. Love, Mom and Dad.*

"My parents were scheduled to be gone for one week. Mrs. Evans stayed with me the whole time. The following Friday afternoon they were due back.

I hurried home from school to help Mrs. Evans with the homecoming dinner. When I walked into the kitchen, Mrs. Evans was seasoning the roast. I made a salad and peeled the vegetables. Mrs. Evans made a lemon ice box pie and an apple pie earlier. While the apple pie cooled in the windowsill, we put the vegetables around the meat in the roaster and set it in the oven.

"The doorbell rang, and she said she'd get it. I heard voices in the foyer, but none that I recognized. I opened the door from the kitchen to the dining room and saw two town officials and our pastor. They'd received a telegram from the Wilson county sheriff in Tennessee that there had been a car wreck. Both of my parents were killed instantly. A few witnesses reported that a truck pulled out in front of my dad at an intersection. Dad swerved, but their car careened off the road and plowed through the guardrail before rolling over into a hundred foot ravine.

"Mrs. Evans was my rock during that period. My home with Lily on South College Street is the home I grew up in with my parents. At first the court wanted to place me in an orphanage. Mrs. Evans stepped in and said she would live with me and be my guardian until I turned eighteen. The court granted the permission. Mrs. Evans also took care of the house the four years I was in the army.

She has definitely been like a mother to me, and a grandmother to Lily."

"I'm sorry, Christopher. It must have been so hard on you. I just can't imagine."

"It was hard, but I had a lot of help. I said I didn't have other family, but Mrs. Evans, my pastor, and just about all of Franklin, Kentucky, became my family. I was truly blessed with all the support. That's why it touched me so much when you told me what the town's people were doing right now. It brought back sad ... but good memories."

Shortly before noon, Henry and Edna approached them in the waiting room. They both looked so excited and were smiling. Henry spoke first. "We just wanted to give you the good news. Our grandson's fever broke about an hour ago. The doctors checked David over, and said they thought he was out of the woods."

Edna was next, and bubbling over in excitement. "Oh, Christopher and Jerilyn, thank you so much for praying with us last night. When we returned to the room, our son had decided to give permission for the doctor to try the penicillin on David. It was administered within thirty minutes, with several doses during the night."

Henry jumped back into the conversation. "We don't know if it was your prayer for our son to make the Lord's decision for David, or just a coincidence, but we think it was the power of prayer. The Lord knew that new drug would help David. We don't know how to thank you for caring about a couple of strangers, but we do appreciate you. If you start preaching again, let us know where, and we'll come and visit." Henry reached in his pocket and pulled out a piece of paper. "Here's our address. We wrote it down for you. Please write to us."

Jerilyn glanced at the piece of paper, and noticed it was a Franklin, Tennessee address, approximately twenty miles south of Nashville.

"This is great news! I'm very happy for you," Christopher said, as he hugged Henry and then Edna.

"I'm happy for you, too!" Jerilyn said, as she too hugged each of them. "I believe in the power of prayer, also."

"All last night when we prayed for David, we prayed for your Lily. How is she?" Edna asked.

Christopher seemed to be unable to form the words to say out loud that she was worse, so he just said, "She's still under observation."

"Well, we're going home now, but we'll be back tomorrow morning after breakfast," Henry said. "We'll come by and visit, and pray you'll be giving us wonderful news on Christmas morning. God bless you both and Lily. We'll continue to pray for

Lily's speedy recovery."

"God bless you both, and David, and his parents," Christopher said, with obvious happiness for all of them.

A few minutes past noon, they watched Dr. Rouse enter Lily's room. Again, he was only in there about fifteen minutes. As he walked toward them, they rose.

Dr. Rouse removed his gloves to shake Christopher's hand. "Well, I can't say there's improvement, but she's not worse either. Everything is about the same as it was three hours ago. Lily seems to be a fighter. This time when you go in, I want you to talk to her with general words of love. Don't say anything about being sick, or how her head looks with all the bandages. Some experts say that the comatose patient can hear. You'll have gloves on, so I have no objection if you want to touch her while you pray for her. I am a complete believer that God works with doctors. The nurses have told me how you two pray. I want you to know I pray for all my patients."

"Thank you, Dr. Rouse. I'll pray for your patients, too ... and for you," said Christopher.

As soon as Dr. Rouse walked away, the aid came to take them to the scrub area. After scrubbing, the aid handed them the clean gowns, masks, and gloves. When Christopher and Jerilyn were ready, the aid escorted them to Lily's room. Two chairs had already been set on either side of Lily's bed. The nurses said they would give them some privacy to speak to Lily. Obviously Dr. Rouse had informed them of his suggestion. One nurse said she'd stand near the door in the event she was needed.

After they were seated, Christopher took Lily's hand. "Hi, sweetheart, it's Daddy. I love you. I hope you can hear me all right. You've been asleep for a long time and it's time to wake up and rise and shine. Mrs. Evans and Ruth miss you. Even though Daisy doesn't speak human, I suspect she misses you, too. Tomorrow morning is Christmas, and I know you'll want to see what's in all those packages under the tree. The Bazells have put something in your stocking. We'll need to go to Christmas Hotel to see what we'll find. Miss Jerilyn is here too, sweetheart, and she'd like to talk to you."

Jerilyn took Lily's other hand. "Hello, Lily. I certainly wish you'd wake up and talk to me. I can't wait to go shopping with you next week. There are always after-Christmas bargains. We need to make a list and see what we want to buy. Why, even that sewing machine might be marked down, so that I can afford it. I'd love to teach you how to sew. I was about your age when my mother began teaching me. I can teach you how to knit, crochet, and embroider a sampler, too. I know samplers aren't made too much anymore, but I made one when I was a little girl. It's been a tradition for the girls in my family for many generations, and I would love to make one with you."

Jerilyn had to pause to clear her throat as she choked up. "You need to wake up soon, Lily, because tomorrow's Christmas Day. I know you can't wait to give your daddy the gift you picked out. I can't wait to see his face, too." Jerilyn paused to smile at Christopher. "Your daddy's a pretty special man, but you already know that." She became aware of Christopher watching her intently. "Well, your daddy wants to talk to you again."

"Hi, sweetheart. Miss Jerilyn and I have to leave for a little while, but we'll be back shortly. We're going to say a quick prayer first."

Christopher and Jerilyn each held one of Lily's hands, and they held hands across her small body and bowed their heads. Christopher prayed aloud.

"Dear Heavenly Father, we thank You for watching over our Lily. We pray Lily will awaken soon. We miss Lily and love her very much. In the name of Jesus we pray ... Amen."

Jerilyn responded with her amen, and noticed Christopher squeeze Lily's hand through his gloves. They rose at the same time. Christopher kissed Lily on the forehead through the mask, and Jerilyn did the same. At the foot of the bed, Christopher took

Jerilyn's hand and walked her to the door. They both turned around in the doorway to look upon Lily before leaving the room, and Jerilyn was painfully aware of the bandaged head.

As they stepped out of the room they thanked the nurse for all her assistance and wonderful care of Lily.

They decided to walk around inside the hospital. Christopher said he had an idea. As they reached the nurses' station, Christopher asked, "Are most of the patients on this floor head trauma patients?"

"Why, yes they are," answered the head nurse. "Most of them are Dr. Rouse's patients. Why do you ask?"

"When we talked with Dr. Rouse, he said he prayed for his patients. Maybe we can visit some of them and do the same. If you could point us to the right rooms, and if it's all right, I'd ... we'd ..." he looked at Jerilyn for confirmation. She nodded yes. "We'd like to pray for them, if they so desire."

"That's a wonderful offer from you two. We definitely don't have enough people willing to volunteer to do this. Some of the churches used to, but none currently do."

The senior nurse gave them a list of room numbers they could go into. For the next four hours they prayed for the comatose, and the patients that were awake. The ones awake thanked them and asked them to call again later if they were still at the hospital. Christopher took out his pocket Bible. He asked each patient if they would like to have a particular passage read to them. Some had not been in a church for a long time. The last man they visited that morning looked to be at least eighty, and his head was bandaged. He asked to have some of the book of Daniel read to him. He said when he was a young boy, he remembered his Sunday school teacher talking to the class about Daniel in the lion's den, and it was his favorite Bible story.

Christopher asked his name, and very softly the man said "Daniel." He looked sheepish as he admitted that was probably why he liked the story so much. After Christopher finished reading selected passages from the first six chapters, Christopher asked the old man if he understood why Daniel in the Bible was so unwavering about his Lord.

Daniel thought a moment. When at last he spoke, it was with careful words. "When I was a boy, I went to a little church in the country. My Sunday school teacher said we should obey God in all situations. Her name was Mrs. Reeder. She said God would never leave us or forsake us. Daniel obeyed God from the time he was young, when he wouldn't eat the king's idol-blessed food or bow down to the king or his idols. Daniel went to the lion's den, but he knew God would deliver him. His steadfast faith in God set him free from the lions. Mrs. Reeder said God would set me free, too. She said that's what I needed to know about Jesus. If I believed He was the Son of God and that He came to me out of love to die on the cross, to save me from my sins, then God would deliver me, too.

"She said I could live forever with Jesus. I remember that lesson so well. I was only ten years old, but it touched me. I now know God was telling me how much He wanted me to come to Him that morning, but I didn't listen when He called. Mrs. Reeder taught us about how God would knock on our hearts. I think she knew I was ready, but I wouldn't ask her to pray with me. To this day, I'm not sure why I kept quiet. I think it may have been because my dad drank a lot, shoved us around ... and my mama. I didn't know what he'd do to me, or my mama, if I told him I'd become a Christian.

"My mama took us to church when she could. Mama had no book learning, but she'd memorized a lot of the Bible. She'd recite the verses to us. I've always regretted not asking Mrs. Reeder to pray with me that day." Daniel looked down, and when he looked back up at Christopher a tear trickled down his cheek. "Now ... it's too late ... for me." He choked the words out with such anguish, it tore at

Jerilyn's heart.

Christopher spoke quickly. "No, Daniel, it's not too late. Do you believe in your heart everything your Sunday school teacher said to you?"

"Yes, I do."

"Do you understand you're a sinner?"

"Yes, yes, I'm a sinner."

"Do you believe Jesus rose from the grave and is now in heaven?"

"Yes, I do."

"Do you want Jesus to save your soul, so you can dwell with Him for eternity?"

"Yes, I do."

"Do you understand that only Jesus can save you from your sins? That it's not anything you can do, but by the grace of God?"

"Yes, I do."

"Let's pray then. I'll begin and you can finish."

They all three held hands and bowed their heads as Christopher led the prayer. *"Dear Heavenly Father, You have just heard Daniel. He desires to become part of our family. He wants You to save his soul. Let Daniel know that he has been forgiven of his sins, and that he can now have peace."*

Daniel took up the prayer. *"Lord, I'm sorry I didn't ask You to save my soul when I was ten. I know now I was afraid of my father. I know my mama is with You, and when I die I want to be with You, too. Please forgive me of my sins. I want to be Your child eternally. Thank You, Lord, for continuing to love me enough to knock again. Amen."*

Jerilyn thought Daniel was about to jump out of the bed in excitement, but he raised his arms and shouted, "Thank You, Lord!" as the tears flowed down his face unashamedly.

Jerilyn would have joined with him, and probably Christopher would as well, but she was afraid they might be kicked out of the hospital for causing such a disturbance. So they simply welcomed Daniel into the family as their brother.

Jerilyn walked out of the room feeling unbelievably happy for the first time in the last twenty-four hours, certain that Christopher shared her joy.

Christopher looked at his watch. "It's five o'clock. Why don't we go get a bite to eat?"

"That sounds good to me. I'm starved for the first time since we've been here!"

They ate quickly and returned to the waiting room. They knew Dr. Rouse made his last set of rounds at about five-thirty in the evening and they wanted to be there.

When they stepped off the elevator, they saw Dr. Rouse leaving Lily's room. He greeted them and shook Christopher's hand. "Your daughter is the same. There's no change in her vitals, and the same amount of swelling is still there. Just continue your prayers, and I will, too. By the way, it's all over the floor that you two led Daniel Cummings to the Lord. He can't stop talking about it. Every time a nurse or visitor walks into his room, he asks if they know Jesus. Did he tell you he's eighty-one?"

Christopher shook his head. "No, but we guessed he was around that age."

"He doesn't have much longer to live. He has an inoperable brain tumor. I can't save his earthly life, but you two led him to the Lord for an eternal life. God bless you both."

Jerilyn stood with Christopher and watched Dr. Rouse in silence as he turned and walked into another patient's room.

****

At six o'clock the aid came for them. They could visit Lily. They washed, suited up, and by six-fifteen were outside Lily's room. In the doorway as they entered, Christopher whispered to Jerilyn, "No, she doesn't look different, but somehow I'm feeling peace with the situation. I don't know if the Lord is healing her or preparing me for her death ... I just know I feel at peace."

They sat on either side of Lily's bed as they did before. They each picked up one of her hands, being careful of her set shoulder, telling her again how much they loved her and couldn't wait for her to awaken. They had so much to tell her. It was Christmas Eve, and Christopher explained to Jerilyn that this was the day he always read the Christmas story after dinner, then they sang hymns while he played the piano.

Jerilyn told Lily again how she looked forward to teaching her sewing, knitting, crocheting, and embroidery. They could get started immediately following Christmas, when she was not working. Jerilyn told Lily she couldn't wait for her to spend time with her own parents and her two best friends in the entire world. "Lily, there are so many people just waiting for you to wake up ... and of course your dog Daisy is waiting, too."

They realized their time was up all too quickly. Jerilyn held Christopher's hand, and the three of them formed their small circle while they both prayed for Lily.

They left the room and took their places in the waiting room. Jerilyn's back began to ache and Christopher found a pillow for her. He pulled up an extra chair so she could prop her swollen feet, and she let out a loud sigh.

He sounded alarmed. "Jerilyn, don't you think you should go home? I can call for someone to pick you up. I think I completely forgot about your condition."

"Christopher, I'm fine," she insisted. "Thank you for your concern, but there's no other place I'd rather be right now. I'm determined to see this through with you. I'm not leaving you and Lily."

"You know, Jerilyn, in these last twenty-four hours I feel as if I've known you for years. I can't believe I just met you ... what ... eight days ago? Does that seem possible?"

"I feel the same way. From the moment I entered this town and Christmas Hotel ... well, all I can say is it's been an amazing journey. I was a broken woman when I arrived here, but I know I've been touched by the hand of God. Christopher, I have the most amazing story to tell you. I told you I rededicated my life last week to the Lord, but I want to tell you how it all came about. I know that the day I was given room number seven, you were astonished. When I saw the CEB crates in the basement, I must admit I was curious. When I asked you why room number seven was never let, you were quite evasive."

She told Christopher how she found the secret drawer that held the diary, and she'd read Carrie Emeline's story of love, loss, and her reunited love with Jesus. She told him the bare details of the life of Carrie Emeline in 1883. "I felt such a sisterhood with this woman I never met, who died thirty-seven years before I was born! We had both become Christians in our youth, although she continued to serve the Lord and I didn't. She was betrothed to her love and I married mine. At the age of twenty, we both lost the men we loved. We both went through depression, and arrived at Christmas Hotel. We both found our Christmas miracle.

"Christopher, there's a peace that settles over that hotel. I truly believe it's touched by the hand of God. The last day Carrie Emeline wrote in that diary was December thirty-first, 1883. She said when our time is up on this earth, meaning her and her parents; she prayed that the Lord would have the right family to continue the traditions of Christmas Hotel. She prayed the hotel would provide blessings and inspiration for people for many years.

"She prayed for the Lord's continued blessings on all the future guests of Christmas Hotel. From what I've seen with the comings and goings of the guests, I know her prayers have been, and are being, answered. The guests of the hotel are touched by God. I know, because I'm one. Carrie Emeline rededicated her life to the Lord, and it touched me so much, that I knew I needed to do the same." She stopped to look at Christopher. "Oh, I'm being chatty. You may not want to hear me run on, and I can do that easily."

"Jerilyn, I love your enthusiasm, and I feel the same way about Christmas Hotel as you and you sister from a different century feel. Please continue. I want to hear everything about your experience."

"Thank you. I prayed for the Lord to help me and return the peace to me I once knew. I asked Him to help me move on beyond my grief, and to know His wishes. I asked Him if He wanted me to give my baby up for adoption, or did He want me to raise my baby. I needed to know His will. I re-read Ken's last letter to me. He told me he'd become a Christian and he wanted me to raise our child to know the Lord. He asked me to rededicate my life to the Lord. I now know I'm meant to raise this baby."

She gently caressed her stomach. Then she spoke almost in a whisper. "When I came here I was in such turmoil over Ken's death that I had lost my joy for this new life growing inside me. Now I realize this precious life is a gift. I will raise my baby with the Lord's guidance. I will not place this child for adoption.

"Carrie Emeline talked about all things being possible with God. You said that to me, and so did Mrs. Bazell. Mrs. Bazell said her daughter died of pneumonia on March twentieth, 1884, but she died happy. She knew her Lord awaited her and she would see Seth again. Mrs. Bazell even commented that Carrie Emeline was probably wondering what was taking her father and mother so long to join her! Mrs. Bazell said that only the Lord knew why the two of them had been kept here so long. She assumed they had just not fulfilled all their purposes. She said that one doesn't know how long one's life will be, and that's why it's so important to ask the Lord for salvation as soon as He knocks. It's never wise to wait. Carrie Emeline was twenty-one when she died. Mrs. Bazell told me Carrie Emeline is buried at Greenlawn, and Ellie and your parents are buried there, too."

"Yes, that's true. Their earthly bodies are there, but we know their souls are with the Lord. Thank you for telling me about Carrie Emeline, Jerilyn. I didn't know much about her. I know the Bazells gave up their lives, as they knew them in Ohio, for their only child. That's what Jesus Christ did for *us*."

One of the nurses approached them with an update. "I'm sorry, but I really have nothing to report. Lily is the same, though, her condition has not worsened."

Christopher asked the nurse if he and Jerilyn could visit Lily around eight or eight-thirty that evening. He explained that was about the time they read the Christmas story every year and then sang Christmas hymns. The nurse telephoned Dr. Rouse, and they were granted permission for the longer visit.

At eight-thirty the nurse told them they were ready for Christopher to read to Lily. Several of the nurses asked to listen in, and Christopher said as many as would fit in the room could listen and sing the hymns with them. He and Jerilyn went to the dressing room to scrub and suit up, and returned to the lobby.

"We're ready," Christopher announced.

All the nurses could not be there at the same time for the reading, so they entered in ten-minute shifts. They came from all the floors, eight nurses at a time. Of course they too had to scrub, put on gowns, masks, and gloves before entering Lily's room. The extra chairs were set up in Lily's room in advance. When Christopher and Jerilyn entered, they wanted to pray first. They asked the first eight nurses if they'd like to join them. Christopher and Jerilyn held Lily's hands and the eight nurses formed a semicircle around them.

Christopher turned to Jerilyn. "I feel so surreal," he whispered. "Such a peace has come over me. I can hear that small voice again, but this time it's saying a verse I know. It's John 14: 27. 'Peace I leave with you, my peace I give unto you: not as the world giveth, give I unto you. Let not your heart be troubled, neither let it be afraid. '"

Christopher began first by reading the story in Matthew from chapter 1 verse 18 through chapter 2 and verse 23. Then he turned in his Bible to the book of Luke. He began with chapter 2 verse 1, and read through verse 20. During the course of the reading, the nurses kept rotating. When he finished the last verse, he closed his Bible. "Now we always sing some Christmas hymns," he explained to the nurses. "Who wants to choose the first hymn?"

The hand Jerilyn held moved slightly. It was Lily's hand. Christopher must have felt it, too.

"Daddy, can ... we sing ... 'O Little Town ... of Bethlehem' ... first? You know it's ... my favorite." The tiny voice struggled with the words.

Jerilyn choked back a sob, while tears streamed down her cheeks. Christopher looked down at Lily, and her beautiful brown eyes looked up at him. His daughter smiled.

"Oh, Lily!" He bent over her, kissing her forehead and cheeks through his mask. He reached out to her small body, careful not to hurt her shoulder or head. "Oh, dear Lord ... *thank You*!" He began to cry huge sobs.

Jerilyn was overcome in the moment, too. She wrapped one arm around Christopher and one carefully around Lily, also crying and thanking God. Behind her she could hear the nurses sobbing. She was aware of them rotating so all could celebrate with them.

Within fifteen minutes Dr. Rouse arrived. He checked Lily and said her vitals were normal and the swelling was gone. He shined the light in her eyes and announced her pupils were equal. He turned to address Christopher and Jerilyn. "I would say the power of prayer was fervent in this room. Both of you never gave up. I wish all my young patients had parents like you two."

Jerilyn wondered if this was the time to explain she was no relation of Lily's, but decided not to say anything for now.

"I want to keep her tonight for observation," Dr. Rouse explained, "and as long as all is well tomorrow morning, I'd say Lily can go home for Christmas under the strictest care of your doctor. You must do exactly as Dr. Beasley says, and keep Lily from getting over excited – even though it *is* Christmas Day!"

Christopher stood and shook Dr. Rouse's hand. "Thank you, Dr. Rouse, for everything."

"I'll see you in the morning," the doctor said.

"Daddy, why ... am I in ... this strange room?"

"Honey, do you remember anything about an automobile when you were playing ball with Ruth?"

"No. We were just playing ... on the sidewalk. Can we go home ... *now*, Daddy? I remember you asking me to wake up. Miss Jerilyn ... promised to teach me how to sew." Lily looked at Jerilyn and smiled, and her voice grew stronger with each word. "You said maybe the sewing machine ... that you want ... might be on sale after Christmas. You said you'd teach me... to knit and crochet and embroider, too." She turned back to Christopher. "Daddy, we need to be home for Christmas. You said Daisy ... and Mrs. Evans and Ruth missed me. I miss them, too."

Jerilyn looked at Christopher in amazement. Lily could remember all their conversations.

"Dr. Rouse, the man you just met, doesn't want you to go home until the morning, sweetheart. Don't worry, Lily, because Miss Jerilyn and I aren't leaving you. We'll be right here. Are you ready to sing 'O Little Town of Bethlehem'?"

"Yes, Daddy. Will you sing, too, Miss Jerilyn?"

"Yes, Lily, I'll sing with you."

The nurses joined in and there wasn't a dry eye in the room. Lily fell asleep while they sang, a slight smile on her face. The nurses checked her eyes and assured Christopher it was a normal sleep. Jerilyn and Christopher each kissed Lily on the forehead through their masks, and the nurses arranged the blanket around her body. Two aids brought in two rollaway beds for Christopher and Jerilyn, and put them on one side of Lily's bed and away from the hospital equipment.

"Courtesy of Dr. Rouse," one said, and smiled.

While they each rolled out a bed, Jerilyn thought for the first time that in coming to this hospital she had finally made it to Nashville. She sat on the edge of her bed. "Christopher, I just thought of something that hasn't occurred to me until now."

He sat on the side of his bed and gave her his full attention.

"I left home to journey to Nashville. How ironic that I have finally completed the journey ... but I've no desire to remain. I do want to meet Ken's family someday soon, and allow them to meet our child. I want my child to know his or her paternal family. However, I know I've found the peace and closure I so desperately sought."

Christopher smiled at her. "I'm happy for you. I'm happy that tranquility surrounds both of us."

Wearily, but contentedly, Jerilyn lay down on her bed as the nurses continued their observations of Lily. Before Christopher lay down on his own bed, he held Jerilyn's hand for a prayer of thanks to God, and they both closed their eyes for sleep.

Chapter Eighteen

Home for Christmas

"Even the youths shall faint and be weary, and the young men shall utterly fall: but they that wait upon the Lord shall renew their strength; they shall mount up with wings as eagles; they shall run, and not be weary; and they shall walk, and not faint."
Isaiah 40:30-31

Thursday Morning
December 25, 1941
Jerilyn awakened around five o'clock. Lily was still asleep, but she saw Christopher sitting up, wide awake. The nurses assured them Lily was just fine. The first thing Christopher and Jerilyn did was to call home and talk to Mrs. Evans and Jerilyn's parents. Mrs. Evans promised to walk over to Christmas Hotel at six o'clock that morning to let the Bazells know, and then make the rounds to tell Ruth and Dr. Beasley.

Jerilyn spoke with her best friends Jack and Emma who offered to pick up the three of them if they could use Christopher's car. Christopher thanked them, and promised to call as soon as Dr. Rouse released Lily. The aids supplied Jerilyn and Christopher with towels and washcloths, so they could freshen up. Jerilyn still had their toothbrushes, toothpaste, and soap in her purse.

When they returned to Lily's room, she was awake.

"Daddy ... Miss Jerilyn!" she squealed with excitement.

Christopher hurried to Lily's side, and then Jerilyn followed, each giving the little girl a kiss and a very gentle hug. There was no longer a requirement to scrub up. The aid said they might be able to put Lily in a wheelchair as her arm was now in a protective sling, and go to the small private dining room down the hall.

At seven o'clock, Dr. Rouse arrived and to everyone's happiness gave Lily permission to go home, on the strictest condition that she was under the care of Dr. Beasley. Dr. Rouse said he would sign the release papers and Lily would probably be out the door by ten o'clock.

Christopher and Jerilyn told Dr. Rouse what Lily remembered while she was comatose. He just shook his head. "I will remember that in the future, for the sake of all my patients and their families. I have long thought we must be careful what we say in the presence of an unconscious person, and this is the proof."

They shook hands and said goodbye.

After calling Jack and Emma to let them know they were ready to leave, Christopher sat Lily in the wheelchair. As they headed down the hall to the private dining room, Jerilyn heard their names and turned around. Henry and Edna had just gotten off the elevator and were walking toward them.

"Is this Lily?" asked Henry.

"It is indeed," Christopher said, with a proud smile.

"Oh, Lily, we're so happy to meet you!" Edna placed her hand on Lily's good shoulder. "You're a beautiful little girl and your parents love you very much."

Jerilyn got the impression Lily was going to correct Edna about her parents, but Henry began to speak and she was clearly taught not to interrupt.

"We wanted to let you know David is going home today. Now, I see Lily may be, too. Is she?" asked Henry.

Christopher smiled with obvious joy. "Yes. Dr. Rouse just released her. He said he'd sign the papers, and we should be leaving by ten. We were just heading to the private dining room for breakfast."

"Well, we wanted to stop and see you before we

left with David," Henry continued. "Remember to write us and let us know when you get a church. Just write us anyway to let us know how you and Jerilyn and Lily are doing. We'd love to hear from you, Christopher."

Christopher nodded. "Thank you. God bless you two, and David, and his parents."

Jerilyn hugged Edna goodbye as Christopher and Henry shook hands.

After breakfast, they still had almost two hours before Lily would be released. They saw from a notice in the hallway that the chapel service was just beginning, and found a seat in the rear with room for Lily's wheelchair. The preacher's sermon was on the birth of Jesus, with the theme being trust.

"Mary had put her trust in the Lord," said the preacher. "She was a virgin, only betrothed to Joseph, and not married yet. Can you imagine how a young girl would be ostracized in that day? Look how shocking it is in our year of 1941 when a young woman has a baby without marriage. Mary had to place her trust in the Lord that all would work out.

"Then there was Joseph's dilemma. He knew the people in town would think he had defiled Mary, but he knew he hadn't. He had to either believe Mary and the angel, that she was indeed with child by the Holy Spirit, or not believe the truth. Joseph had to place his trust in God.

"Then there are the people through all the generations from the day of Jesus' birth through the present. Are you going to place your trust for salvation and eternal life in the arms of Jesus? Will you trust Him to forgive you of your sins? Will you trust He is the Son of God and He has a plan for you?"

Jerilyn remembered the day she met the Bazells, and when Mrs. Bazell said, 'As long as evil exists, these things will happen.' It was evil that bombed Ken's ship. Every day she read more accounts of what happened that fateful day.

God had a plan for her, for sure. She understood He promised to never leave her or forsake her. She realized she could place her trust in the Lord, and He would protect her and her baby's future. *Thank You, Lord.*

Before leaving the hospital, they visited with David and prayed for the comatose patients one last time. They entered Daniel's room and discovered his bed was empty, scrubbed clean, and his belongings removed. They asked at the nurses' station and were told Daniel passed away early that morning. Even though they did not have a chance to say goodbye to Daniel, they knew they would see him again. They knew where his soul now dwelled.

Christopher looked at Jerilyn and smiled.

"When we are absent from the body we are present with the Lord," he said. "That's a paraphrase of 2 Corinthians chapter five, verse eight. It was one of my mother's favorite scriptures. She would quote it when a loved one died, so I would know that someday we would see them again. You know, I can't keep from thinking the Lord caused good things to happen out of Lily's accident." He turned to Lily and smiled. Jerilyn knew that what they said to her at this age, she would probably remember the rest of her life.

Christopher knelt down in front of her wheelchair. "Lily, I can't tell you the depths of emotion that I ..." he looked up at Jerilyn, "and Miss Jerilyn went through when you were injured. I'll tell you more about it when you get home and are feeling up to it. We met many people in this hospital that needed prayer. Miss Jerilyn and I want you to understand the power of prayer, and God can make good things happen out of bad. Do you remember the Romans 8: 28 verse I taught you?"

"Yes, Daddy, 'and we know all things work together for good to them that love God, to them who are the called according to his purpose.'"

"That's right, sweetheart. God made many things good come out of your accident."

When they arrived back at Lily's room, Jack and

Emma were there to greet them. They gently hugged and kissed Lily, and then more robustly hugged Jerilyn and Christopher.

"The nurses say Lily is all checked out and ready to go home," said Emma. "Dr. Beasley will be calling at your house every day to attend to her dressings and to make sure all is well. Now we just need to gather the things from her room."

When they walked in, Jerilyn saw two large pots of flowers. One was a Poinsettia, and the card said, "With love from the patients at Protestant Hospital." The other was a pot of lilies, and the card said, "God bless you, Lily. From Dr. Rouse, the nurses, and aids at Protestant Hospital."

Jerilyn cried when she saw the messages, and Emma did too.

Lily just squealed in excitement. "I've never received flowers, and now I have two pots of them! This is my first Christmas present. I hope I get the main Christmas gift I asked for," she said, as she looked from her father to Jerilyn.

Jerilyn felt her face blush. While Christopher and Jack gathered Lily's pots of flowers, Jerilyn pushed the wheelchair. They walked to the nurses' station first and hugged the nurses and aids goodbye. They thanked them and told them to tell the others thank you.

****

They arrived home, and within minutes well-wishers began to pour in. Some brought presents for Lily and some brought more food. Mrs. Evans laughed. "Well, I don't think I need to cook a Christmas dinner. I do believe we have enough food for all of us to last this week and well into January! I've already frozen most of the casseroles, and what wouldn't fit in your freezer, is in mine and the one in Christmas Hotel."

Dr. Beasley arrived and checked Lily over thoroughly. He expressed surprise at the speed of the little girl's recovery, although he pointed out that there was still much healing ahead, and they had to take great care of her.

They opened their presents, with Lily propped up on the couch, so she could not move herself too quickly, whether by accident or design. Dr. Beasley explained this was the first of many visits, and agreed Lily could stay in the room for a short time, but she was definitely not to be allowed to get overexcited.

Jerilyn gave her parents the drawing she bought of the square and Christmas Hotel. Lily gave her daddy his sweater, for which she received a very careful hug and kiss. Jerilyn had crocheted scarves for Christopher, Captain and Mrs. Bazell, Mrs. Evans, Nettie Sue, and Lily, using the yarn she purchased when she shopped with Lily. Nettie Sue dropped by to welcome Lily home, and Jerilyn gave Nettie Sue her scarf. Nettie Sue had made Christmas cookies for Lily and a night gown for Jerilyn.

Christopher gave Lily a Jeannie Walker doll. Jerilyn read it was all the rage for little girls that year. She thought it even resembled Lily with its curly dark brown hair and brown eyes; resembled her before the hospital had shaved her head. Earlier, when Christopher told Jerilyn he had bought the doll for Lily, Jerilyn fit in some time to sew a dress for it. Lily looked ecstatic with her new doll and the dress Jerilyn made. Mrs. Evans received perfume and bath powder from Christopher.

The last two gifts to be opened were for Jerilyn. Christopher picked her gift from under the tree and set it on the floor in front of her chair. It was a large package, and when Jerilyn finished unwrapping her gift she sat back in wonder. It was the sewing machine from *Draper and Darwin's Dry Goods* on the square. She looked at Christopher, and a tear escaped her eye and ran down her cheek. She tried to wipe it away before he could notice.

Lily looked as though she was about to stand up, and Christopher had to calm her and ask her to keep still. When at last Jerilyn spoke, it was with difficulty. "Christopher ... I didn't expect this ... it's too much. I don't know what to say." She looked at her parents, Emma, and Mrs. Evans, but they just smiled warmly.

Lily's eyes, so recently lifeless, now gleamed. "Just say you like it," she said.

Jerilyn looked at Christopher. "I like it. Thank you, Christopher. I promise to teach Lily how to sew with this machine."

He leaned down and kissed her on the cheek. "You're welcome, Jerilyn. I also appreciate you teaching Lily. I think she's as pleased with the gift, as I was giving it to you. Lily helped me find the right store selling the sewing machine you liked, and she wanted to give you something, too. Lily, with your permission, I'll hand it to Miss Jerilyn."

Lily stayed where she was, but with her good arm pointed to the last gift under the tree. Christopher retrieved it and handed it to Jerilyn. She unwrapped the package, and found maternity patterns and material for a blouse and skirt.

"Daddy said you're going to have a baby, Miss Jerilyn. He said you would soon begin to look like Ruth's mom before Ruth's baby brother was born. She got pretty fat, so I told Daddy you were going to need some fat people clothes."

The whole room burst out in laughter. "Oh, Lily, honey." Jerilyn sat beside Lily and gave her a very gentle hug and a kiss on the cheek. "Thank you, sweetheart. I *am* going to need some fat people clothes. This is a very thoughtful gift."

At that, Mrs. Evans said, "Let's eat! We just need to heat up the food and set the table." Everyone pitched in, and as neighbors dropped by, they were invited to share in the feast.

Christopher carried Lily to her chair and everyone, except Lily, stood and formed a circle around the table while Christopher asked the blessing. "*Dear Heavenly Father, we have so much to be thankful for this Christmas. Thank You for Jerilyn arriving in Franklin instead of Nashville. We've all come to love her. Thank You for Christmas Hotel. The blessings You shine on that hotel continue to inspire all who visit, and to understand the importance of knowing Your Son. Thank You for the Bazells who continue the tradition of Christmas Hotel and why it was built. Thank You for bringing Jerilyn's parents and friends to Franklin so we could all get to know them, and love them, too. Thank You for Mrs. Evans who is a mother to me and another grandmother to Lily. Thank You for returning my daughter Lily to all of us, and may she soon be back to full health.*"

At that, Christopher choked up, but Jerilyn squeezed his hand for encouragement, enabling him to continue. "*Thank You for allowing Jerilyn and me to pray with the patients at Protestant Hospital. Daniel and David in particular were the Christmas miracles, outside of Lily, that I'm most thankful for. God bless our friends and family as we finish this day of Your Son's birth. Help us know that like the motto of Christmas Hotel, every day should be a special testament to Your Son. In the name of Jesus Christ we pray ... Amen."*

The others agreed, adding their amens. Then they formed a circle around Lily, and prayed for a special blessing on the little girl.

Chapter Nineteen

Eighty Years of Love

"Trust in the Lord with all thine heart; and lean not unto thine own understanding. In all thy ways acknowledge him, and he shall direct thy paths."
Proverbs 3:5-6

Thursday Evening
December 25, 1941
Jerilyn agreed with Christopher it would be a good idea, at least for now, to set the sewing machine up in the bedroom Mrs. Evans used when she spent the night. That way Jerilyn knew she could give Lily lessons when she wasn't working. There really was not a great deal of space in her room at Christmas Hotel.

At eight o'clock it was Lily's bedtime, and Jerilyn insisted she help put her to bed. Jerilyn carried Lily upstairs, helped her brush her teeth, put her gown on, and with great care tucked her into the bed.

Jerilyn picked up the brush on the vanity, and sat on the bed beside Lily. "One day soon you will have lovely hair again, and I promise I'll brush it for you."

Lily giggled. "This will be fun. It will be like when I have a slumber party at Ruth's house. Ruth's mother brushes our hair for us, too. She's nice like you, and pretty, but I think you're prettier."

Jerilyn blushed but managed to say, "Thank you, Lily."

Jerilyn looked up as her mother came in and sat down on Lily's other side. She took the brush from Jerilyn. "I remember brushing your hair for you, Jerilyn, when you were little. I think our best time of the day was our nighttime ritual. Sometimes it's sad for me you've grown up. I miss this time together."

"I do, too, Mom."

Lily cut into the conversation, "Both of you can come over any night and brush my hair when it's all grown back. I'd like that. I wanted a mommy for Christmas, but if you two came over every night, I'd almost have a mommy and a new grandma."

Jerilyn glanced at her mother, and caught her perceptive eye.

Christopher walked into the room with a discrete cough to announce his presence. "Well, what a lucky little girl you are, Lily. You have the help of two beautiful women looking after you.

What story do you want read tonight, sweetheart?"

"A ... how about ... *The Long Winter.* I like to hear about Laura Ingalls and her mommy and her daddy and her sisters."

"Good choice, sweetheart."

"Mrs. Morgan, will you stay, too?" Lily asked.

"I will, Lily, if you want me to stay."

"Miss Jerilyn, will you read the story?"

"I would be happy to read to you, Lily."

Christopher removed the book from the shelf and handed it to Jerilyn. Mrs. Morgan took a seat in the rocker to watch. Jerilyn had not completed more than six pages when Lily fell sound asleep. She and Christopher tucked her in on both sides and each kissed her goodnight.

Jerilyn noticed her mother had her eyes closed too, but not in sleep. She knew her mother so well. She was praying. A moment later Christopher turned off the light on Lily's nightstand, helped Mrs. Morgan to her feet, and the three walked downstairs.

Jerilyn allowed Christopher to help her into her coat, and then he did the same for Mrs. Evans before he slipped on his own. They wrapped the scarves around their necks, Christopher and Mrs. Evans wearing the ones Jerilyn had crocheted for them. They then added their hats and gloves, and the women were ready for Christopher to walk each of them home.

"Thank you for watching over Lily while I walk Mrs. Evans and Jerilyn home," Christopher said to Jerilyn's parents and Jack and Emma, while stuffing the gifts for the Bazells into a shopping bag.

"It's our pleasure, Christopher," Mr. Morgan answered. "Thank you for opening your home to us so we can spend time with our daughter."

"Don't forget I have to work at Mr. Blakely's diner in the morning," said Jerilyn. "I hope to see all of you there. I'm sure Christopher will be there with Lily."

"Yes, Lily and I will be there – if she feels well enough to go out in the wheelchair. It'll be nice getting our routine back in order."

He walked Mrs. Evans home first. She just lived a few doors from Christopher. Jerilyn continued with Christopher on to Christmas Hotel, and came upon the bench on the square facing Christmas Hotel.

"Jerilyn, if it's not too cold for you, would you mind sitting with me on this bench? I really would like to speak with you in private."

"All right. Actually it's not so cold, and the wind's not blowing. It's such a beautiful clear night." She looked up. "I think I can count a thousand stars."

They sat on the small bench in the pool of light from the gas lamp above them, and for a moment remained silent, observing the beauty of the stars. Jerilyn recognized the bench. "I sat here when I first arrived in Franklin. That day seems as though it was months ago and not days. So much has happened. I was so scared to walk in Christmas Hotel and beg for charity. I did not know then that my Christmas miracle was waiting for me."

Christopher waited for her to finish and then cleared his throat. He turned toward her, so he could look into her eyes. "Jerilyn, please hear me out before you say anything. I want you to know the two days we spent together at the hospital meant a lot to me. I know you didn't have to stay with me, but I must tell you I appreciate the love and concern you showed for Lily. I thank you for the prayers, not just for Lily, but for everyone we met at the hospital. I think we make a great team."

He reached for her hand and held it in his. "I fell in love with you during those two days," he said softly. "I think I was beginning to care a great deal for you even before the accident, but now I'm sure. You're a very special lady and I can't imagine spending the rest of my life without you. I don't think it was a coincidence your purse was stolen and you wound up here. We were meant to meet. We still don't know why all those ships were bombed in Pearl Harbor. We don't know why so many Americans died, but I do know God is love, and the bombing was caused by the evil in the world. God gives people freewill and they can use it for evil or good."

Jerilyn blinked back tears as Christopher continued. "I've grown up a great deal in my thinking since Ellie died. I know that when bad things occur, God has a plan to help us through any situation. I know you will always have love for Ken, as I have for Ellie. That's something we should never forget ... something we must cherish. Now here, today, on Christmas 1941, I declare to God and the world that I love you, Jerilyn. If you will marry me, I promise to love you and cherish you all the days of my life. I also, promise to love your child, as I do Lily."

At this point the tears in Jerilyn's eyes that had threatened to spill now streamed down her face. He took out his handkerchief and wiped her eyes. He then wrapped his hands around her cheeks. "Will you marry me, Jerilyn?"

Jerilyn looked into Christopher's eyes and saw such love and longing. She wrapped her hands around his. "Christopher, when you asked if you could court me when I was ready, I must say I was nervous. I couldn't imagine courting another man so soon after Ken's death. You are right that God had a hand in our meeting. I was also meant to stay at Christmas Hotel in room number seven, Carrie Emeline's room. I was meant to find that diary. My life has been a whirlwind of emotions since I arrived here. God definitely had a plan that began long before we were ever born. I love you and Lily, too. I would be honored to become your wife."

He drew her face to his and kissed her ever so gently. "Jerilyn Marlene Seifert, you've made me a very happy man. I know a little girl named Lily who is going to be very happy to have a mommy. It's too late to tell her tonight, and I don't think over breakfast is such a good idea. Let me arrange for you to have tomorrow night off from your hostess duties. I'm sure my assistant can host the dining room. We have plenty of food at home, so we can turn tomorrow night into a celebration. What do you think about a New Year's Eve wedding in the chapel at Christmas Hotel? Hopefully, I can get Pastor Palmer to officiate. Lily shouldn't be too disappointed not having a mommy on Christmas Day. After all, every day is Christmas at Christmas Hotel!"

Jerilyn dabbed at her eyes with Christopher's hankie. "That will give me time to sew a special dress for the wedding. My suit and dresses are getting mighty tight. Lily might like a new dress, too. She can help for her first sewing lesson. I'll just need to take it slow with her until she's stronger. We can pick out the material on Saturday morning. I'm sure my mother and Emma will help with the sewing next week, when I'm at work. I'd like to tell my parents and friends before we make the announcement to Lily tomorrow night. Tomorrow morning at breakfast, when I see them, I can ask them to come to Christmas Hotel after my shift at Mr. Blakely's diner. You can invite Mrs. Evans to dinner at your home Friday night. Then we can make a small wedding guest list."

"My darling, you can invite anyone you wish." He kissed her again before they left the bench.

When they walked into Christmas Hotel, Captain and Mrs. Bazell sat together on one of the sofas in the lobby. Jerilyn looked at Christopher and smiled.

"Let's tell them," said Christopher.

"I agree. Let's do."

They handed their gifts to the Bazells and sat on the sofa across from them, while the Bazells unwrapped their presents. The Bazells thanked them for the thoughtful gifts.

"We have something to tell you," Christopher began.

"We're getting married," finished Jerilyn.

"That's wonderful!" Mrs. Bazell said, with obvious happiness but perhaps no great astonishment. "Best wishes to you both."

Captain Bazell rose to his feet, along with Christopher, and shook Christopher's hand. "Congratulations, son. You chose a good woman."

"I agree. Thank you, sir. We would like to marry here in the chapel on New Year's Eve."

"We can't say we're surprised," said Mrs. Bazell. "Now, go get your gifts from under the tree."

Christopher found the two small packages with each of their names and handed Jerilyn hers. They opened the gifts and Jerilyn held a gift box with a man's gold band inside. Christopher held a box with a woman's gold band and a second ring with a sapphire and three diamonds. They stared at the rings, and then each other, not knowing what to say.

Mrs. Bazell smiled at them. "We felt the connection between you two almost since Jerilyn first arrived. I think we knew before you two did. However, we knew you would have a lot of obstacles before you found your way to each other." She looked at Jerilyn. "I am sure you know God had a plan for you, and by now you know how He has been working in your life. I knew for certain when you told me about Carrie Emeline's missing diary.

"Captain Bazell and I did not want you to be burdened with the expense of buying rings, and we have no living child to leave these rings. We want you to give the rings you are holding to each other, but only if you so desire. We do not want you to feel obligated."

Jerilyn noticed for the first time that the Bazells' rings were not on their hands. They had given them their precious possessions. "I would be honored to wear your rings," she said.

Christopher echoed her response.

Mrs. Bazell's face lit up. "I still remember the day Jacob placed that sapphire and diamond engagement ring on my finger. It was on Easter Sunday 1860, a year before the war began ... the Civil War, mind you. He was nineteen and I was seventeen. I really don't know the age of the engagement ring. I only know it belonged to Jacob's grandmother. These rings have never left our fingers since the day we married after church on Sunday, June 10, 1860 ... that is until now. Captain Bazell went off to war in April, 1861. However, he wasn't a captain until three years into the war. He did not come home much during those four years, but I am glad to say he was home long enough for us to conceive Carrie Emeline." She smiled with love toward her husband. "Carrie Emeline was born April 14, 1863. She was the joy of our lives for the nearly twenty-two years God loaned her to us.

"We never know what life has in store for us. If

we knew the future, we would all probably live in depression or fade away and cease to exist. God never gives us more than we can handle, and always makes a way for us, no matter what happens. I know you two will always love your first spouses, but we all have enough room in our hearts to add another. You will find this love different, not better or worse, but different. It will be a more mature love."

Captain Bazell added, "Never go to bed angry without working out your differences, and do not neglect telling each other daily that you love the other." He patted his wife's hand. "Right, Mary?"

With her other hand, she patted his hand in return. "Right, Jacob."

Jerilyn smiled as she witnessed over eighty years of love and devotion between the Bazells. *I can only imagine*, she thought as she looked up at Christopher.

Chapter Twenty

Passing the Torch

"And be renewed in the spirit of your mind; and that ye put on the new man, which after God is created in righteousness and true holiness."
Ephesians 4:23-24

Wednesday Morning
December 31, 1941
The week had been a whirlwind of activity. Last Friday, December twenty-sixth, Jerilyn and Christopher held the engagement celebration. Lily hugged Jerilyn. "I'm getting my mommy."

Tears pooled in Jerilyn's eyes. "Yes, you are, sweetheart."

"May I call you Mommy now?"

Jerilyn looked to Christopher and he nodded.

"Yes, you may, Lily."

As planned, Jerilyn told her parents and her friends Emma and Jack the day after Christmas in the afternoon at Christmas Hotel. They were ecstatic for her. Jerilyn worried they would think she made a decision too soon after Ken's death.

They assured her they did not look at it that way. They said they felt she had lived more like a matter of years than days this past month. They made it known how they had observed her comfortable but loving relationship with Christopher and Lily, and they were pleased for her. Jerilyn told them what the Bazells had said about their coming marriage, and without hesitation they agreed. They expressed amazement at the beautiful engagement ring when they saw it. Jerilyn's mother whispered to Jerilyn that she had noticed she was not wearing her rings from Ken.

"I've put them away to save for my child," Jerilyn said, holding her stomach. "He or she may want them someday for his or her future marriage. Christopher can now place this engagement ring on my finger tonight at the party."

By Saturday, December twenty-seventh, Dr. Beasley said Lily was making great progress, and could walk for short distances, although for most of the time she must still be taken around in the wheelchair. She had complained of the cold air on her head once the bandages were removed, and said she couldn't wait for her hair to grow back. All she had now was a small dressing to cover the wound, so Jerilyn knitted her a woolen hat to keep her head warm, and she sewed pretty scarves for indoors.

Jerilyn helped Lily shop to pick out material for their new dresses with the help of Jerilyn's mom and Emma. They began work making the dresses on Jerilyn's Singer sewing machine, with Lily watching in awe as the material whirred through the mechanism.

On Sunday, December twenty-eighth, after the service with Pastor Palmer, Jerilyn was rebaptized, per her own request, in the chapel at Christmas Hotel by Christopher. She desired to renew her baptism vows in a public affirmation of faith. Although she had been baptized after she was saved at age eleven, she desired her friends and family to recognize her rededication to the Lord, and share her testimony to celebrate her new life in Christ that she had neglected for so many years. Several hotel guests and people from Franklin came and stood at the back to watch.

On Monday afternoon, Jerilyn, Christopher, and Lily made two giant cards. One was a thank you card for Dr. Rouse, the nurses, and the aids at Protestant Hospital. With the help of Jerilyn and Christopher, Lily drew Christmas pictures with her good hand and wrote thank you. Jerilyn and Christopher included a note of thanks. The other giant card was for the patients at the hospital, letting them know that Christopher, Jerilyn, and Lily were praying for them to get well soon.

Christopher and Jerilyn walked to the post office to mail the giant cards, and pick up the marriage license at the court house on the square.

On Tuesday, between jobs, Jerilyn found time to spend with Lily sewing their dresses. In the mornings when Jerilyn was at work, she knew her mom and Emma were working on the dresses with a little help from Lily, and both dresses were complete by Tuesday evening.

On Wednesday morning before the wedding, the Bazells summoned Christopher and Jerilyn to Christmas Hotel. Judge James was there also. The Bazells informed Christopher and Jerilyn they were signing over the ownership of Christmas Hotel to them as their wedding gift. They said they could not think of anyone better to take over this magnificent hotel and continue its mission. They would still be there every day to greet the guests, but the hotel would now belong to Christopher and Jerilyn.

Jerilyn turned to Christopher in amazement, and they thanked Captain and Mrs. Bazell for this unbelievable gift.

Later, walking with Christopher to his house, Jerilyn quoted Carrie Emeline's last words in her diary on December 31, 1883. *"When our time is up on this earth, I pray You will bring the right family to continue the traditions of Christmas Hotel. I pray this hotel will provide blessings and inspiration for people for many years."*

Jerilyn looked at Christopher. "I wonder what Carrie Emeline would think if she knew her diary would help change lives fifty-eight years later. I hope she knows her dream will live on."

Christopher hugged Jerilyn close to his side and kissed her cheek. "I think she'd be pleased.

Chapter Twenty-One

New Year's Eve

"Wherefore they are no more twain, but one flesh. What therefore God hath joined together, let not man put asunder."
Matthew 19:6

Wednesday Evening
December 31, 1941
Pastor Joseph Palmer said there was nothing better he would like to do on New Year's Eve than to marry Christopher and Jerilyn. At six o'clock the guests gathered at Christmas Hotel. Christopher and Jerilyn only invited a few for the small chapel.

The thirteen invited guests were Captain and Mrs. Bazell, Jerilyn's parents, Lily, Mrs. Evans, Mrs. Palmer, Jack and Emma, Mr. and Mrs. Jonathan Blakely, Nettie Sue Harris, and Dr. Beasley. Jerilyn asked Emma to be her matron of honor and Lily to be her flower girl. Christopher asked Jack to be his best man.

Jerilyn sat on the bed in room #7 to wait her music cue to descend the grand staircase and enter the chapel. She smiled at her mother and Emma who were waiting with her, along with Lily holding her little basket containing lilies and rose petals to spread on the floor of the chapel, on which Jerilyn would step. Jerilyn wore the dress she made that week with the help of her mother and Emma. She stood and viewed a final look in the full-length mirror at her floor-length silk dress, pale blue with delicate white lace on the sleeves and at the throat. She bought a pattern with an empire waistline to help conceal the growing bump on her belly. Lily's dress matched hers, except it was pale pink, with a special cap of beautiful lace Jerilyn had made for the occasion.

Laughing, they discussed the old, new, borrowed, and blue. For new she wore her dress, which covered the blue requirement, too. For both borrowed, and old, she would hold Carrie Emeline's 1883 diary that Mrs. Bazell gave to her for this occasion. She realized her mother was asking her a few questions. "What do you feel you have learned and what has God taught you since you left home? What have you lost and gained?"

Jerilyn pondered the questions before she answered. Looking straight into her mother's eyes she said, "I lost my innocence and naiveté, and I've learned life isn't always fair." She turned to Lily and smiled. "What I've gained is an inner strength I didn't know I had. I know with God's help I can do anything. I am blessed with a wonderful family and friends ..." in mid-sentence she turned to Emma and smiled, "who have prayed for me and loved me." She turned back to Lily, "This is what I want to teach Lily and my new baby." She reached out her arms to Lily, and Lily stepped into them. "I love you, Lily."

"I love you, too, Mommy."

The music began in the chapel. Lily had asked earlier if they could play Christmas hymns for the wedding, since every day was Christmas at Christmas Hotel. Jerilyn and Christopher agreed that Christmas hymns would be perfect. Jerilyn walked to the top of the staircase and watched as her mother and Emma descended the steps side-by-side. Lily followed behind holding the basket of petals. Jerilyn had slipped the basket handle through Lily's sling, so she could spread the petals with her good hand.

Jerilyn felt excited rather than nervous. Her mother and Emma entered the chapel. She knew her mother would take a seat on the front row aisle seat. Emma would be taking her place at the front of the chapel opposite Christopher and Jack. She could see Lily at the chapel entrance, already scattering the petals. After spreading the petals in the aisle, Lily would then take a seat on the front row with Mrs. Evans.

Jerilyn watched as her father strode into the doorway. He smiled up at her, and she returned the smile. Jerilyn knew he was the only one who saw her as she descended the staircase.

As Jerilyn stepped across the threshold of the chapel, she took her father's arm, and the guests rose. She stopped and looked around in awe. She had not imagined a scene as beautiful as this. The only lights were candles held by the guests, and candles on the organ where Pastor Palmer's wife sat and played the hymns. Holding her father's arm, Jerilyn walked toward the front. Christopher watched her and they locked eyes lovingly. When she and her father reached the front of the chapel, he gave her hand to Christopher. She and Christopher held hands as they continued to gaze into each other's eyes, while Pastor Palmer asked the guests to be seated. Then Pastor Palmer began the ceremony.

"Dearly beloved, we are gathered together here in the presence of God – and in the face of these witnesses – to join together this man and this woman in holy matrimony, which is commended to be honorable among all men; and therefore is not by any to be entered into unadvisedly or lightly but reverently, discreetly, advisedly and solemnly. Into this holy state of matrimony, Christopher and

Jerilyn now come to be joined. If any person can show just cause why they may not be joined together, let them speak now or forever hold their peace."

There was silence in the chapel.

Pastor Palmer continued. "Marriage is the union of husband and wife in heart, body, and mind. It is intended for their mutual joy and for the help and comfort given on another in prosperity and adversity. Through marriage, Christopher and Jerilyn make a commitment together to face their disappointments, embrace their dreams, realize their hopes, and accept each other's failures. Who gives this woman in marriage to this man?"

"I do," Jerilyn heard her father answer loudly.

Pastor Palmer resumed. "Marriage is an act of faith and a personal commitment as well as a moral and physical union between two people. It is a moral commitment that requires and deserves daily attention. Marriage should be a lifelong consecration of the ideal of loving kindness – backed with the will to make it last.

"Do you, Christopher Joseph Wright, take Jerilyn Marlene Seifert to be your wife? Will you live together after God's ordinance, in the holy estate of matrimony? Will you love her, comfort her, honor and keep her, in sickness and in health, for richer, for poorer, for better, for worse, in sadness and in joy, in sickness and in health, to cherish and continually bestow upon her your heart's deepest devotion, forsaking all others, keeping yourself only unto her as long as you both shall live?"

Christopher answered, "I will."

"Do you, Jerilyn Marlene Seifert, take Christopher Joseph Wright to be your husband – to live together after God's ordinance – in the holy estate of matrimony? Will you love him, comfort him, honor and keep him, in sickness and in health, for richer, for poorer, for better, for worse, in sadness and in joy, to cherish and continually bestow upon him your heart's deepest devotion, forsaking all others, keeping yourself only unto him as long as you both shall live?

Jerilyn made sure she answered clearly. "I will."

Pastor Palmer said, "Please place the rings in my hand."

Emma and Jack each handed him a gold band.

Pastor Palmer continued. "May these rings be blessed as the symbol of this loving unity. May these two find in each other the love for which all men and women yearn. May they grow in understanding and in compassion."

Pastor Palmer handed Jerilyn's ring to Christopher. "Christopher, you may place the ring on Jerilyn's finger with your words to her."

"Jerilyn, I give you this ring to wear with love and joy. As a ring has no end, neither shall my love for you. I choose you to be my wife this day and forevermore." He slipped the gold band on her finger.

That morning, Jerilyn had given him the sapphire ring to return to her finger at this moment. He reached into his pocket, retrieved the sapphire and diamond engagement ring, and placed it against the gold band.

Pastor Palmer handed Christopher's ring to Jerilyn, "Jerilyn, you may place the ring on Christopher's finger with your words to him."

"Christopher, this ring I give to you as a token of my love and devotion to you. I pledge to you all that I am and all that I will ever be as your wife. With this ring, I gladly marry you and join my life to yours." She slipped the gold band on his finger.

Pastor Palmer resumed. "In the presence of God and these witnesses, I now pronounce you man and wife. Christopher, you may now kiss your bride."

Jerilyn felt a great excitement and happiness as Christopher bent and kissed her lips. They turned to their family and friends, who were all smiling joyously. Jerilyn looked to her mother who was crying, and noticed her father wipe a tear. Lily hurried to them, and Christopher bent down and carefully picked her up. Jerilyn and Christopher walked out of the chapel hand in hand, with Christopher holding Lily in one arm, toward their future.

Chapter Twenty-Two

The Birth

"There shall no evil befall thee, neither shall any plague come nigh thy dwelling. For he shall give his angels charge over thee, to keep thee in all thy ways."
Psalms 91:10-11

Four and a half months later
On Friday morning, around three o'clock May 15, 1942, Jerilyn's labor began. Jerilyn waited a couple hours before awakening Christopher, timing the contractions by the bedside clock. Eventually she shook his shoulder. "Christopher, I think it's time to get Dr. Beasley."

Christopher rushed to put on his shirt and pants.

"Try to stay calm," she added, feeling far from calm herself, "and please come straight back. Don't wait while Dr. Beasley gets dressed. Just tell him to hurry. Oh, and please stop first to ask Mrs. Evans to come."

By the time Christopher returned home, Lily was standing in the upstairs hall, jumping up and down with joy. "My baby brother or sister is coming! My baby brother or sister is coming!"

Mrs. Evans left the bedroom and came into Christopher's view. She called downstairs to Christopher, explaining that she had placed an old quilt under Jerilyn and laid out clean towels for the doctor. She had water heating on the stove, to pour in the small tub to wash the baby.

"I'm going downstairs now with Lily," Mrs. Evans said.

Christopher climbed the stairs two at a time and entered their bedroom. Every couple of minutes Christopher asked Jerilyn if she was all right. Jerilyn knew that in the back of Christopher's mind he must still be remembering what happened to Ellie.

"Please, God, please take care of Jerilyn," he prayed aloud as he held her hand.

Dr. Beasley arrived and asked Mrs. Evans to help him, and told Christopher to wait downstairs. The doctor must have seen Christopher's anxiety and decided it would not be beneficial to Jerilyn if he stayed.

He walked Christopher into the hallway, but Jerilyn could hear the doctor's deep, confident voice. "Christopher, please try to stay calm. What happened to Ellie was very unusual. Jerilyn will be just fine. Go sit with Lily and be in happiness for this new life for which God is blessing you and Jerilyn to raise."

Thirty minutes later, the baby lay in Jerilyn's arms. Mrs. Evans hurried to the top of the steps. "You have a son, Christopher. I'll bring him out as soon as I wash him. Jerilyn is fine," she added hastily.

Jerilyn could hear Lily shout out, "I have a baby brother!"

Then the contractions started again. Five minutes later, Mrs. Evans hurried to the top of the steps. "Christopher," she called excitedly, "you have a daughter, too!"

Within thirty minutes Jerilyn asked Dr. Beasley to have Christopher and Lily come in. She heard their eager voices as they climbed the stairs. Dr. Beasley met them in the doorway. "Congratulations, Christopher. Jerilyn is feeding the babies and your family is just fine. Don't tire them out. When the babies finish feeding, let all three have some rest. I'll return in a couple of days to check on them. I'll just let myself out. You're in good hands with Mrs. Evans."

"Thank you, Dr. Beasley."

Christopher held Lily's hand when they approached the bed. Jerilyn was exhausted, but she managed a smile as Mrs. Evans finished combing her damp hair. "Come see your son and daughter,"

Jerilyn said to Christopher, who was struggling to hold back the tears of joy.

Mrs. Evans had already pulled up an extra chair for him and Lily. “Christopher, you and Lily visit with Jerilyn while I go prepare us all some breakfast,” she said.

Lily sat wide eyed as she watched both babies nurse at Jerilyn’s breasts. Mrs. Evans had dressed them in gowns and wrapped them in their blankets.

“We certainly didn’t plan on two babies,” Jerilyn said, with some concern as she watched Christopher’s face.

Christopher must have seen her anxiety and seemed quick to dispel any notion she might have that he wasn’t pleased. “No, we didn’t,” he answered. “So, I suppose we need to go shopping for another cradle and later another crib.” He looked at her affectionately, and with complete sincerity said, “Jerilyn, I couldn’t be more pleased.”

“Daddy, may I touch them?”

He laughed, “Sure, sweetheart. Just be very gentle with them for a while. Maybe in a few days you can even hold them.” He lifted her to the babies and she touched each little cheek.

“They’re so soft!”

He set Lily back on his lap in the chair. “I think we should name our son Kenneth,” he said. “That way his biological father will live on through his name."

"Thank you, Christopher. I'd like his middle name to be Elliot. It sounds like the masculine for Ellie. Our son will be the combination of the names of our first loves."

"Kenneth Elliot Wright," said Christopher. "It has a nice ring to it. I like it. What about our daughter?"

"I would like to name her Carrie Emeline. Although I never knew her, she's very special to me."

"She is to me, too," Christopher said with a smile. "Well, Lily, meet your brother and sister, Kenneth Elliot and Carrie Emeline Wright."

"I can't wait to tell Ruth," Lily said happily. "I've got a baby brother *and* a sister ... all at one time!"

"Right now we need to let mommy, Kenneth Elliott, and Carrie Emeline have some rest." He placed the babies together in the cradle and kissed Jerilyn. "I love you, Jerilyn."

"I love you, too, Christopher."

****

Eight days later, on a beautiful sunny morning, the happy family was ready to visit the Bazells at Christmas Hotel. They placed the babies in the new stroller, and along with Lily walked down South College Street toward the square. As they turned the block and walked down West Cedar Street, they encountered the town's people along the way. In front of *Gillespie Dry Goods*, two elderly ladies stopped them so they could view the tiny twins.

Another couple who were leaving Simpson County Bank stopped them again. Each time Lily would say, "They're my baby brother and sister!" She showed no sign of jealousy. Her love and admiration sparkled in her eyes, along with her bouncing up and down with each step. The old men sitting on the benches around the square, whittling, stopped their whittling long enough to wave to the family. Finally, they arrived at North Main and East Cedar Streets.

Guests leaving the hotel also wanted to see the babies. All of them had met Christopher during their stay. Jerilyn had not worked at the hotel the last month of her pregnancy, and had quit the diner upon Christopher's suggestion after they married. After all, they now owned Christmas Hotel, and wanted to devote their efforts to maintain the hotel's mission ... and of course raise their children with love and care.

The Bazells were expecting them and were seated in the lobby. Jerilyn and Christopher picked up the sleeping babies and carried them to the sofa where the Bazells sat.

"May we hold them?" asked Mrs. Bazell.

"We would be privileged," said Jerilyn.

Christopher placed Kenneth Elliot in the arms of the old Captain, and Jerilyn placed Carrie Emeline in Mrs. Bazell's welcoming arms. Jerilyn watched as a tear trailed down the old lady's face.

"She's beautiful," said Mrs. Bazell softly. "Carrie Emeline would be pleased you chose her name. I know I am." She looked over at Kenneth Elliot. "I like your son's name, too. You chose well. We have a gift for each baby. Lily, if you will look under the tree, you will see two packages, each marked with Kenneth Elliot or Carrie Emeline."

Jerilyn opened the gift boxes from *Mallory Jewelry Store*. Each box contained a silver spoon, with the initials KEW and CEW beautifully engraved on each individual spoon.

"We also have one more gift, and it's for you, Jerilyn." Mrs. Bazell handed her a box containing all the diaries belonging to Carrie Emeline. "I want you to have these, and later on you can give them to her namesake. You and I have both read the 1883 diary. Someday you can tell your daughter the story regarding your miracle at Christmas Hotel."

"Thank you, Mrs. Bazell. I will always treasure these diaries. You know I feel as though your daughter was my real sister, and not just as my Christian sister. I will always feel a kinship to her. Sometimes I feel as if I really knew her."

"Well, someday you *will* meet her. Just holding

your daughter makes me feel close to my daughter again. It brings back many memories." Mrs. Bazell touched Carrie Emeline on the cheek and kissed her forehead. "Thank you for bringing the babies to us. I now feel as though our purpose has been fulfilled."

Epilogue

"But the God of all grace, who hath called us unto his eternal glory by Christ Jesus, after that ye have suffered a while, make you perfect, stablish, strengthen, settle you. To him be glory and dominion for ever and ever. Amen."
1 Peter 5:10-11

Mrs. Bazell's last words to Jerilyn were prophetic. The couple were found one week later in their bed, he with his hand on hers. Dr. Beasley said they both died peacefully in their sleep. It was as if she knew she and her husband had finished their mission on earth, and they could now go to their eternal reward.

At their funeral, Pastor Palmer said the Lord was not going to separate this amazing couple in death or eternity. The two most likely were welcomed into heaven by Jesus with the words, "Well done, good and faithful servants." They were now reunited with their beloved daughter Carrie Emeline.

The day after the funeral, Christopher and Jerilyn ordered the double monument for the Bazells.

Captain Jacob Barnabas Bazell
June 15, 1841 – May 29, 1942
God-fearing Man, Husband, Father, and Friend

Mary Eve Winters Bazell
August 1, 1843- May 29, 1942
God-fearing Woman, Wife, Mother, and Friend

The week following the Bazells' funeral, Christopher, Jerilyn, and Lily, placed the babies in the stroller and walked to Greenlawn Cemetery. The Bazells' marker had been installed the day before, and they laid flowers on the graves of Christopher's parents, Ellie Wright, Carrie Emeline Bazell, and Captain and Mrs. Bazell.

Jerilyn's life was not the only one renewed by the Lord. Christopher again became the minister that he was called to be. He performed the weddings in the chapel at Christmas Hotel. He preached on many Sundays throughout the year for the guests, and held early morning Bible studies for them. He was the chaplain on duty every other Friday night at Protestant Hospital in Nashville, and on-call whenever a chaplain was ill. He wrote to Henry and Edna, who at least once a month traveled up from Franklin, Tennessee to Christmas Hotel, spent the weekend at the Wright family home, and listened to Christopher preach in the chapel.

Jerilyn resumed her duties, Monday through Friday, as the hostess for the evening meal in the dining room. Lily and the babies stayed in room #7 with Mrs. Evans during the shifts Jerilyn worked.

Lily received her wish for a mommy.

Daisy had a litter of four pups.

The End

About Saundra Staats McLemore

Saundra Staats McLemore is a member of the American Christian Fiction Writers (ACFW) and the Ohio chapter of the ACFW. Saundra is also a member of Landmark Baptist Church in Dayton, Ohio. After thirty-three years, Saundra is recently retired as President/CEO of McLemore & Associates, Inc., a nationwide sales and marketing business she built in 1984.

Saundra's passion has always been history, and she enjoys reading historical Christian fiction. Saundra's novel *Abraham and Anna* was endorsed by two of her favorite authors: Richard Paul Evans (author of *The Christmas Box*) and Jeanette Oke (author of the Love Comes Softly series). Saundra has two series published: The two-book inspirational eighteenth century Staats Family Chronicles and the six-book inspirational Christmas Hotel series. Saundra is currently writing her ninth novel: *For the Love of Ali*.

Born and raised in the state of Ohio, Saundra is married to Robert, and Anthony is their only child. The other two members of the family are the cat Charley, and the mixed-Treeing Walker Coonhound Sadie.

Author's Notes

Christmas Hotel was inspired by an article from January, 2008, in the *Franklin Favorite,* a newspaper in Franklin, KY. The article spoke about a diary left behind in the now razed Keystop Motel in Franklin, KY. The diary, dated 1873, possibly belonged to a young girl named C.E. Bazell from Rock Camp, Ohio. An Ohio assistant librarian traced the diary to a girl named Carrie E. Bazell who lived in Rock Camp with her parents until the late 1800s. Carrie Bazell died March 20, 1884 at the age of twenty-one, according to a brief obituary. It's amazing how a small newspaper article can stir one's heart, as this story did mine.

Penicillin was used by several hospitals in the United States in 1942. It was in 1941 scientists purified the substance and established it was both effective in fighting infectious organisms and not toxic to humans. By March, 1942 enough penicillin had been produced to treat the first patient in the United States, Mrs. Ann Miller, in New Haven, Connecticut. Therefore, I "jumped the gun" a bit by using penicillin in the story in December, 1941. (Referenced by Wikipedia)

In 1918, an influenza epidemic ravaged Nashville, and out of this crisis the currently named Baptist Hospital was established. Originally known as Protestant Hospital, it was incorporated on December 12, 1918.

Debt grew quickly during the Great Depression and during World War II. As a result of the ongoing financial difficulties, the ownership of Protestant Hospital was transferred to the Tennessee Baptist Convention in 1948 and became Mid-State Baptist Hospital. The name would later change to Baptist Hospital, on December 17, 1964.
(Referenced by Wikipedia.)

Dr. L.F. Beasley was a practicing physician in Simpson County, Kentucky from 1934 until he retired in April, 1975. He served in WWII beginning sometime in 1942. He made house calls until he retired, delivered many babies, and conducted many surgeries. He died in 2011 at the age of 103. His mind was good; he drove his car until age 99, and played golf into his late 90's! He did not like his given names, therefore, he went by his initials L.F., and so I will not reveal his given names either. (Information provided by his daughter Barbara Beasley Smith of Franklin, Kentucky)

Other "visitors" to the story were my husband Robert E. McLemore's parents Nettie Sue Harris McLemore (Currently resides in Bowling Green, KY) and James (Booker) E. McLemore (now deceased). Also, Roy Harris (deceased) was Robert's grandfather.

Mt. Vernon Church is an actual church in Simpson County. My husband's great-grandfather Bailey Peyton Harris around 1873 or 1874 donated the land for Mt. Vernon Church. Nettie Sue Harris McLemore, the granddaughter of Bailey Peyton Harris, is still a member.

There were approximately 2,350 deaths when the Japanese bombed Pearl Harbor on the morning of Sunday, December 7, 1941. Nine U.S. ships were sunk and twenty-one ships severely damaged. Most of the deaths occurred on the U.S. Arizona, which received a direct hit.

Psalms 40:1-3
I waited patiently for the Lord; and he inclined unto me, and heard my cry. He brought me up also out of a horrible pit, out of the miry clay, and set my feet upon a rock, and established my goings. And he hath put a new song in my mouth, even

praise unto our God: many shall see it, and fear, and shall trust in the Lord.

2 Corinthians 12:9
And he said unto me, My grace is sufficient for thee: for my strength is made perfect in weakness. Most gladly therefore will I rather glory in my infirmities, that the power of Christ may rest upon me.

A sneak peek of the second book in the series, *Christmas for Lucy*. Enjoy!

Chapter One

Bullet

"He shall cover thee with his feathers, and under his wings shalt thou trust: his truth shall be thy shield and buckler."
Psalm 91:4

Bowling Green, Kentucky
9 pm Wednesday, December 1, 1954
Lucy lay curled in a ball near the fountain in Fountain Square Park. The tears that had flowed so freely earlier that day were now just dirty streaks on her thin face. She gingerly tugged on the threadbare coat to try to gain some warmth. Although a hand-me-down from Hazel her older cousin, for once Lucy was happy that the coat was too big for her. She could wrap it around her body like a blanket. However, the dress she wore was too small, and the hem was well above her knee. She wore Hazel's discarded boots, but no socks. Lucy fled the apartment in such a hurry she forgot her hat, scarf, and gloves.

Before she entered Fountain Square Park, she stopped by the Methodist Church on State Street. There was a Nativity scene out front, lit with floodlights. She knelt by the manger that held the baby Jesus. On occasion her mama attended this church along with Lucy, and even more often since August. Lucy knew about the baby Jesus. Her Sunday school teacher Mrs. Scott taught her class about this precious baby. Mrs. Scott explained that He could save her from her sins and would protect her. Lucy did not understand sin, but she did understand the need for protection.

Lucy stared into the manger and studied the rubber doll representing the baby Jesus and the statues of Mary and Joseph. Wrapped in a blanket, a sweet smile on the doll's face, and the statues of Mary and Joseph gazing on with love; the scene depicted what Lucy had been told about Jesus. Jesus was loved. Lucy wanted to be loved.

She bowed her head and prayed aloud softly. "Dear baby Jesus, I'm scared. Do You know my mama died this morning? Do You know today is my eighth birthday? Do You know that nobody cares about me? Do You know I'm all alone in the world? Do You know that I have no home? Will You help me, baby Jesus? Will You protect me? Is there somebody out there who will love me? I'm so cold." As she prayed, the tears streamed down her face.

No one came by. Lucy was indeed all alone.

The short, but poignant plea was prayed a couple of hours ago, and now Lucy lay shivering near the old fountain. Burying her head in her coat to seek as much warmth as possible, she resembled a scared turtle returning to the protection of its shell. She snuggled close to one of the shrubs around the fountain. The shrub provided some shelter, so at least she had a bit of protection from the cold damp air as she peered out from her coat and gazed up at the heavens. It was a clear evening, and she could see the stars. Her mama would tell her to count sheep in her head to go to sleep. Tonight she counted stars. With the leaves long gone from the park's trees, her eyes feasted on the clear view. By the time she counted approximately fifty stars, she was asleep.

In the middle of the night Lucy woke up shivering. In the shadows a dog slowly walked toward her. Her heart beat faster in panic. Too frightened to run, she pulled her coat back over her head. If she couldn't see the dog, maybe he couldn't see her either. Feeling movement at her back, she tentatively peeped out from her coat. The dog, now lying down beside her, rested his head on her body. Cautiously, she reached out to pet him. He licked her hand and laid his huge head back down on her. Feeling safe with the dog within fifteen minutes

Lucy had stopped shivering and was asleep.

In those minutes just before the sun peaked over the horizon, she awakened. The dog still lay by her side, protecting her and warming her body. Sporting a rough, shaggy coat he was a good-sized dog and stretched out longer than Lucy. Her mama used to take her to Lerman's Department Store on the square where they sold the new televisions. Immediately after school, Lucy stopped on the way home, and also on Saturday morning when the store turned its television channel to The Roy Rogers Show. Every child in town, who didn't have a television, had his or her face pressed up against the store-front window. Bullet, Mr. Rogers's German Shepherd dog, and prominent in every episode, looked just like her new friend and protector. Lucy always wanted a dog, but her mama said they couldn't afford one, and had no space to keep one within their small apartment above *Tandy's Billiards*. Since this dog looked just like Bullet, she decided that's what she'd call him Bullet. Remembering her prayer last night to the baby Jesus, she said aloud, "*Thank You, baby Jesus, for sending me Bullet.*"

A light snow continued to fall. Thirsty, she stuck out her tongue to catch the snowflakes. Her mama told her she shouldn't drink the water in the fountain, because it was tainted. Bullet lifted his head and licked her cheek. She laughed and hugged him. Raising herself to a sitting position, she saw a man walking toward her in the dim morning light. The man weaved along the walkway, stumbling every now and then. Holding a paper bag in one hand, he stopped long enough to bring the bag up to his mouth. When he was within ten feet of her, she could smell him. He smelled just like Uncle Otto and Aunt Eula Mae when they came home late at night. It was a sickening smell and Lucy did not like her aunt and uncle when they had that smell. Sometimes they yelled at her or hit her. She stayed with them when her mama worked at night at the theater. They lived across the hall in an apartment over the billiard parlor, too.

The man stopped when he saw her, but did not come closer. A deep guttural growl in Bullet's throat grew louder and more menacing. The man stumbled away as quickly as possible, nearly tripping over his own feet. Lucy hugged Bullet to her. "Thank you, Bullet." She planted a big kiss on his massive head.

Lucy's stomach growled. She was hungry. She had not eaten since the previous morning, and even that was nothing substantial: just a piece of toast and some milk. She stood and Bullet stood beside her, tail wagging. He watched in anticipation of her next move. She looked to the east and had her first glimpse of the sun, just barely tipping above the horizon. Lucy stretched her arms, pulled her coat tighter, and looked around the park and the businesses on the square, but she saw no activity. She needed to relieve herself. There was a privy behind the billiard parlor and Lucy began to walk in that direction. Bullet followed.

When she returned to the park, she sat on the bench to view the fountain and wait; however, she really had no idea why she was waiting. As she stroked Bullet's head, she spoke aloud. "Mama, why did you have to die?"

She looked up to the heavens and the tears began again.

Christmas for Lucy
will be available December 06, 2018.

Made in United States
Orlando, FL
05 December 2021

11155152R10141